Gambler's Dawn

For many years Doc Spengler has been hunting down his father's killer. Now the trail leads him further west into Bent's Crossing, Colorado, where he is taken on as house gambler by Whispering Williams, the owner of the Silver Bullet saloon.

By chance, Doc stumbles across the murderer only to find that he is a highly respected citizen and the father of the girl to whom Doc has taken more than a passing fancy. When the man is killed and Doc is arrested for the crime, Williams helps him to break out of jail.

The final pursuit and confrontation to rescue the girl who has been taken hostage makes for a breathless and exciting tale of the old West.

SLOW.   HCA

HIGHCLIFFE LIBRARY
GORDON ROAD
HIGHCLIFFE 3106
TEL: HIGHCLIFFE 272202

2 3 NOV 2009
1 0 DEC 2009

2 3 MAY 2006   - 3 JUN 2008
- 8 JUL 2006 2 0 SEP 2008
              2 0 NOV 2008
3 1 AUG 2006
2 8 DEC 2006   1 3 MAR 2009
              2 5 AUG 2009
1 9 NOV 2007 2 6 OCT 2009

Dorset County Council

Gambler's Dawn

Dale Graham

stern

DON

ISBN-10: 0-7090-7896-X
ISBN-13: 978-0-7090-7896-8

Robert Hale Limited
Clerkenwell House
Clerkenwell Green
London EC1R 0HT

Typeset by Derek Doyle & Associates, Shaw Heath.
Printed and bound in Great Britain by
Antony Rowe Limited, Wiltshire.

ONE

HIGH STAKES

'I'll take two!'

In the blink of an eye, a duo of pasteboards flicked across the green-baize table. Slick Warriner was well named. Sometimes his blurred dealing left other players wondering whether the cards had indeed originated from the top of the deck. As yet nobody had found just cause to challenge the house gambler.

'A pair it is then,' responded the nattily dressed dealer to the newcomer sitting opposite. 'Here's hopin' fer your sake they work some magic.' The oily smirk on the house-man's thin face held no trace of sincerity. He effortlessly retrieved the discards and slipped them to the bottom of the deck.

Typical of the breed that inhabited saloons in cow towns at the Kansas railhead of Newton, Warriner adopted an easy-going, casual manner in an attempt to bluff his opponents. A red-silk vest, lurid and bright, glittered beneath the sputtering coal-oil-lamp that hung above the card-table. The loud-checked suit had seen better days as well.

Aaron Spengler, otherwise known as Doc, had only arrived in Newton that afternoon. A granite-faced man in his mid-twenties, his flinty expression gave nothing away. The Ramrod was his first call.

A wide open town, Newton had gained the unenviable reputation in that year of 1873 as being the wickedest town in the Union. It was often said that *There ain't no Sundays west of Newton.* Such a town offered easy pickings for men in Doc Spengler's walk of life. Not that the tall stranger had any intention of robbing his opponents. But towns like Newton were bread-and-butter to a hard-nosed gambling man. And Doc had every intention of making his skills with the pasteboards count.

He casually skewered the dealer with cool appraisal. Not a muscle moved on Doc's stony mask. Feelings and emotion had no place at the card-table. This was serious business. Only the diamond-hard blue eyes exhibited any life-force.

A slight frown cracked the marble exterior, barely perceptible. The guy was doing well. A little too well. Doc considered himself a good poker man. He had learned to make a steady if unremarkable living at the tables.

But this dude had him worried. He seemed to have a second sight. Knew every card he was holding. Doc's stack of chips had noticeably shrunk.

Impassively, he surveyed the other players.

The one to his left was clearly a cowboy. New duds and a slicked down short-back-and-sides told a familiar story. Recently off the trail and anxious to have some fun, the greenbacks amassed from three months' pushing a herd up the Chisholm were burning a hole in the poor sap's pocket. Give him a few days, a week at the most and it would all be gone. Too much hard liquor and an itchy pecker would see him bumming a ride back to Texas. And the whole caboodle would begin all over again.

To his right a banker, or perhaps a lawyer. A successful businessman who enjoyed the good things in life, especially fine whiskey if the large purple snout was anything to go by. Puffing constantly on a large Havana, the guy's russet visage was ready to burst. He had lost heavily and it showed, a hundred bucks down at least.

Then there was Slick Warriner. The beaver-skin derby stuck at a rakish angle gave the house dealer the aura of a foppish caricature; someone you most assuredly wouldn't trust with your wife, or your winnings.

The gambler's waxed moustache twitched.

'You in or out, Tex?' he asked.

Scratching at his black curly thatch, the cowboy threw down his hand.

'This table ain't pushin' Lady Luck my way,' he scowled grabbing his new Stetson. 'Reckon I'll find me a new game. One that gives a fair shake to the punter.'

'You callin' this a rigged game, mister?' snarled Warriner frostily. His right hand slid menacingly towards his vest-pocket. Doc could just discern the slight bulge that doubtless concealed a tiny derringer.

'No way,' asserted the Texan, hands raised in a placatory gesture. 'You're just too good for the likes of me.' He quickly stood and left the saloon.

The gambler shifted his attention to the flustered businessman. Thin eyebrows were raised in a probing expression, long sinewy fingers toying with the cards.

'Lady Luck sitting on your shoulder then?' he quizzed, not bothering to disguise the implied sarcasm.

Dabbing at his sweat-beaded brow with a white linen handkerchief, the rotund gent huffed and spluttered, piggy eyes fluttering between the sniggering dealer and his own hand.

'Well?' snapped Warriner impatiently. 'You gotten the bottle?'

'Maybe I also had better call it a day,' stuttered Red Nose, stubbing out the cigar. 'Perhaps tomorrow the cards will be more receptive.'

Without acknowledging the banker's flustered retirement, Slick Warriner turned to his opposite number. Here he at least recognized a worthy adversary.

For Doc, that was when the penny dropped. The gambler's coal-black orbs, deadly as a rattler, held the key. Each time cards changed hands Warriner's eye appeared to lift, as if he was studying the wall behind Doc's chair, thinking on his next move. Was it a ploy, a ruse to disguise some nefarious scam?

Doc Spengler had come across cheats before. Not many. Such gamesters received short shrift when exposed as frauds. Tarring and feathering before they were run out of town was a common response from those on the receiving end. Although he could recall more than one occasion when instant gunplay had terminated the varmint's shenanigans.

On this occasion there was only one way to find out if his suspicions had any basis of truth.

'I'll take one more,' he said, coughing to hide the hesitant crack in his voice.

'A man after my own heart,' quipped the dealer, flicking out a replacement card. 'Now to the real business.'

Doc struggled to maintain his classic poker-face. A bead of sweat dribbled down his neck. There it was again. The raised eye followed by a brief nod. Nothing of any note to the unwary. But everything to a like-minded professional.

An accomplice was feeding him. Avidly studying his hand, Doc's mind whirled like a spinning-top, trying to figure how to play this new development. His heart pounded in his chest. He needed to learn the score without alerting Warriner that he was on to his skulduggery.

'This game is thirsty work,' he averred firmly. 'I need a drink.'

He pushed his chair back and stood, slipped the poker-hand into his vest-pocket, and nonchalantly shouldered a path to the crowded bar. With deft precision, he slid between the horde of raucous cowboys who were enthusiastically dancing a merry gig to the hammering piano. At the same time, his steely gaze surreptitiously lifted to the veranda at the rear of the saloon. A staircase led up to the first floor which was lined with doors.

At first he could see nothing untoward. His face creased into a perplexed frown. There had to be some way that Slick Warriner was reading the cards.

Then he saw it.

A slight movement of the curtain at the end of the landing. Narrowing eyes focused intently. He could just discern a hole in the heavy velvet with a tube poking through. Then he perceived a brief glint as hazy light reflected off glass.

A telescope!

Using a spyglass, the accomplice could easily read the cards of everybody facing the dealer. Prearranged signals then indicated what hand a potential sucker was holding – one finger for an ace, two for a king and so on. It didn't matter how they worked it. Cheating was cheating.

Doc Spengler clenched his fists, the knuckles white with suppressed anger. If there was one creature he loathed on God's earth it was a card-sharp. The lowest of the low. His jaw tightened, the gleaming white snappers bared defiantly.

As he cast a sly glance towards Warriner, Doc's features hardened further. The skunk was so confident of his deception that he was even smiling openly towards the hidden collaborator. He knew that, whatever hand was held by his opponent, he couldn't lose.

Doc sank his drink in a single draught. His dander was well and truly up. And there was only one route to take from here. Catching Warriner's caustic eye, he made an earthy sign regarding his need for a bodily function. The gambler nodded expressively.

He slipped out through the side door at the far end of the bar, marked: *Privy This Way*, and emerged into a back alley. Most of these double-storey saloons had a rear stairway. This one was no exception. He slipped effortlessly up to the first floor.

At the top, he carefully tried the outside door. It opened noiselessly. As he entered a corridor sounds of ribaldry filtered up from the drinking-den below. The corridor was empty, for now. Drawing his pistol, a Remington-Rider 1863 double-action, he tiptoed down the gas-lit passage, praying that none of the doors on either side opened.

At the end the corridor swung to the right. A balustraded landing complete with curtain overlooked the main body of the saloon. Muted laughter drifted from behind one of the closed doors. Some drover having himself a high old time in the sack. Tendrils of blue smoke drifted up from below.

And there he was. A spindly weasel seated on a low stool, left eye glued to the telescope. Since he was in such an exposed position it was obvious that the saloonkeeper was in on the scam, doubtless creaming off his own illicit percentage of the take.

Doc sucked in his breath, gripped the revolver's long barrel, and edged forward. Halfway between the corner and his quarry a board squeaked loudly. Alerted, the weasel turned.

'Who in the blue blazes are you?' he quailed on seeing the raised gun.

'I'm the sandman come to put you to sleep,' grunted Doc as he leapt forward slugging the guy across the side of the head. It was a solid hit. The little runt slumped to the ground unconscious. Blood dribbled from a cut above the critter's left ear. Doc grabbed the telescope and slid it into his jacket-pocket. He smiled at the thought of how he intended to confront the thieving card-wielder.

Doc was a big, raw-boned man in the prime of life, well-toned and solidly built. The conniving skunk below held no fears for him. Now well into his forties, Warriner had spent too much time in the smoke-ridden atmosphere of frontier saloons. He was flabby and out of condition.

Unlike most travelling gamblers, Doc believed that moderation in all facets of life produced its own rewards – a quick mind, calculating brain and swift reactions when danger threatened. Especially when cheating card-sharps needed a blunt reminder concerning the rudiments of their profession.

As was the case now.

Returning from his supposed visit to the privy, Doc sat down opposite a grinning Warriner. A blank expression once again cloaked the younger man's raw-boned exterior.

'Feeling better now?' enquired Warriner, his cadaverous mush smirking in vicarious anticipation.

'You could say I never felt better,' replied Doc lightly. 'Now. Let's play poker.'

It was an hour later. Slick Warriner had lost all his polish. In fact he was looking decidedly jaded and grey around the gills. Gone was the twisted leer, the cocky demeanour. All the chips had shifted from his side of the table to his opponent's. A glazed look of shock had stunned the gambler to silence.

What had gone wrong? Where was Magpie? Why wasn't the little critter passing him the reading?

As Doc had figured, cheating jaspers like Slick Warriner couldn't hold their end up when it came to playing in a legit game. He had him by the short and curlies. And now that the bastard was cleaned out, he could play his final hand.

Slowly, he removed the telescope from his pocket and rolled it across the green cloth. Warriner's eyes popped, his jaw hung open. Now he knew. But still he tried to bluff his way out of the dead-end street, denying any underhanded chicanery with a poker-faced vehemence that might have cowed less resolute adversaries.

'Don't give me all that eyewash.' Anger and indignation creased Doc's lean façade. 'Your rat-arsed pal is taking a well-deserved nap.' He jerked a thumb towards the veranda.

Warriner's face dropped. He knew there was no point denying his duplicity.

'W-what yuh g-gonna do?' he stammered, hypnotized by the spyglass.

Doc's reply was barely above a whisper.

'If I catch sight of your mangy hide in Newton after today, I'll gun you down on the spot like the sidewinder you are.'

Warriner's greasy mug twisted, his hand sliding towards the vest-pocket.

'Don't even think on it, mister,' advised Doc holding the other with an even regard. 'You wouldn't make it.'

Wanner hesitated. The up-and-over derringer was so close. Should he?

But the snake-eyed glower stayed his hand. He pushed back his chair and made to leave the saloon, resetting his hat at a jaunty angle.

'There'll be another place, stranger. And next time . . .'

Doc interrupted the implied threat with a terse retort.

'Any time, card-sharp. Now get out afore I lose my temper.' The holstered Remington had jumped, seemingly of its own volition, into its owner's right hand. It poked menacingly at Warriner's gut.

The exposed cheat backed off, making a hasty exit on to the street. Doc Spengler sighed with satisfaction. He scooped the large stack of chips into his black Stetson and sauntered over to the bar.

'Cash these in, bartender,' he said brightly. Then in a louder voice: 'The next ten drinks are on me.'

There was a hurried scuffling of chairs as thirsty men surged to the long bar elbowing and barracking each other. Free drinks in Newton were a rare event.

Doc smiled, moving down the polished mahogany to avoid the headlong rush.

TWO

MEDICINE SHOW

On the opposite side of Newton's broad thoroughfare known as Drover's Alley, and some three blocks east, stood the Crystal Theatre. Originally a standard saloon with all the accoutrements such an establishment was expected to provide, an adjoining extension had been built to offer a diversity of stage productions to entertain the clientele further.

All the latest musical extravaganzas from New York were now able to reach the newly emergent mid-west cattle towns of Kansas by means of the rapidly spreading railway network. Shows of a cultural nature vied side by side with the popular, more earthy distractions. All designed to capture the hard-earned greenbacks that a constant flow of Texas beef was furnishing. Shakespearean productions one week, an eye-catching songstress warbling popular ditties the next.

One of the latter was standing in front of the impresario's large desk, hands provocatively clamped on her hips.

'So what be wrong with my act then?' she demanded of the smarmy dude lounging behind the desk. A powerful lilting brogue left no doubts as to her Irish ancestry. To further emphasize her disquiet, the singer arrogantly flicked at the pink feather boa encasing her elegant neck.

Ginger LaPlage knew her worth. The French *nom de théâtre* gave her a more refined image. She might not be the best soprano, nor even the most accomplished dancer, but the cheering that followed her spirited rendition of all the latest music hall favourites was no figment of the imagination. Indeed, she had performed two encores before the closing promise to an ecstatic audience that she would be on stage again the following night at eight o'clock prompt.

The curtain descended to the accompaniment of ear-battering applause.

In the wings a flustered stage-hand had quickly wiped the broad smile from her lips. He had nervously informed her that the boss wanted a word. And that he was none too pleased. This was Ginger's fourth night at the Crystal. And each performance had received more acclaim than the last.

The singer knew exactly what the score was. And she had no intention of playing this leech's game.

Dandy Beau Merrick presented a smooth silky exterior. From his perfectly tailored suit down to the highly polished patents, his whole demeanour oozed the conceited affectations of a pompous slug. He even wore perfume. Overweight and on the small side, he made up for a lack of the more masculine attributes that his female companions normally preferred by means of a fat bill-fold.

It worked every time. A few crisp dollar bills waved at

the appropriate time had always opened far more than doors for Beau Merrick. And in addition to the Crystal, he was also a partner in the Ramrod. Life was a bowl of cherries.

From the very first he had assumed that Ginger would succumb to his lecherous suggestions for off-stage entertainment. The singer had come across many such creatures on her travels. They all received the same short shrift. Some gracefully accepted the put-down. Others, like this oily clown, tried to pull rank.

'It has been drawn to my attention,' he intoned haughtily, thumbs tucked into his bulging cummerbund, 'that your songs are not to the taste of certain ladies in Newton. They have complained that the lyrics are somewhat, shall we say, indelicate.'

He was referring to the Ladies Temperance League. An organization dedicated to closing down the gin-palaces and cat-houses that were, in spite of their spirited efforts, flourishing in Newton. The good ladies were, however, not without influence. Many were married to local dignitaries active on the town council. Ordinances and by-laws had already been brought into force restricting hours of opening and entrepreneurs like Beau Merrick were anxious not to ruffle the fine feathers of these matriarchs.

Not that they had ever been known to enter personally establishments of ill repute such as the Crystal. He was playing a bluff hand.

'Nobody out front complained,' countered Ginger, glaring wildly at the manager. Her flaming tresses jiggled like a Thanksgiving bonfire. An accusatory finger, its long nail painted a bright scarlet, stabbed at the manager. 'And ain't it the goddamned truth that tonight I gave two

16

encores?' Ginger could cuss and swear as good as any trail hand when she had a notion. 'If that's bad showmanship, then you ain't no connoisseur of what the punters be wanting.'

'I have my licence to think of. And these ladies can petition the mayor to shut me down.' Merrick bristled and postured to hide his discomfort. This feisty gal sure was a hells'-a-poppin' livewire, and some looker to boot. Why couldn't she just accept the situation like all the others.

'Don't give me that load of cow-clap,' snapped Ginger, now well and truly riled. 'There wasn't one of these so-called ladies out front tonight. Nor any other night for that matter. This is just 'cos you can't have your own way.'

'Not at all,' responded a red-faced Merrick attempting to regain the initiative. 'I can only—'

'Cut the crap, you overgrown tub of lard. You couldn't get inside my petticoats, so it's the push I'm being given.'

Merrick leapt to his feet, his paunchy torso wobbling, eyes bulging with indignation. Nobody, not even the star of the show, which this gal certainly wasn't, talked to him in that way. Globules of spittle gurgled from the spluttering mouth as Merrick did his best to play the outraged employer.

'Out!' he ranted, short arms windmilling frenziedly. 'Out, do you hear? I have never been so insulted in all my life. And by a two-bit singer.' Merrick returned the prodding finger routine. His face had darkened measurably to a wholesome maroon, almost matching the colour of Ginger's fiery locks. 'I will see to it that you never find any more work in this town.'

'Think I care. This scabby dump ain't no New York. And to be sure, you ain't no gentleman.' Ginger screwed her finely-sculpted features into a snooty pout.

Now that the die was cast she was trying to give as good as she got, knowing that the next day she would be out of work. Not an exciting prospect for a single woman, especially one in her profession. Many people viewed female stage-entertainers as little better than saloon girls. That was clearly the case with this gut-bucket.

Head held high, she swung abruptly on her four-inch heels, almost toppling over in the process, then made for the door.

'There's plenty more where you came from,' sniggered Beau Merrick, lighting up a fresh cigar. 'It would have been easier all round if you'd been more . . . co-operative, shall we say?'

'You say what you like,' countered Ginger. 'But I wouldn't be touching the likes of you with a ten-foot bargepole.' Without waiting for a reaction she slammed the door extra hard and stamped off down the corridor and out into the bustling night.

Too late she realized that she hadn't been paid. A momentary pause. Should she go back? The toad owed her four nights' money. And let him have the pleasure of seeing her beg? Not a chance! Ginger LaPlage had her pride even if it did mean she would be forced into a midnight flit from her boarding-room at the Ramrod.

That would serve Dandy Beau Merrick right. She smiled at the notion of at least getting one back on the snivelling rat.

The bottle of blue label was half-empty, and Doc Spengler was still leaning against the polished mahogany bar. A scantily clad damsel smiled provocatively down at him from the wall behind, her obvious assets displayed for all to admire. Hard liquor dulled the pain inside, the inner clamour that frequently consumed him.

Gambling and whiskey were fine bedfellows. A good win and you celebrated. A loss and you drowned your sorrows. And so it went on. Town after town. Maybe some day, he would find the time to settle down, raise a family, engage his agile brain in the pursuance of a proper job.

Certainly not the life he had grown up around. From as far back as he could recall, the Spenglers had been involved with the running of a travelling medicine-show. He smiled at the thought. Most of the time it was fun, and certainly enabled you to see the country. As a boy, Aaron Starkey Spengler had been dubbed 'The Mighty Atom'.

A scowl twisted the handsome features. How could such quick-witted, clever parents have missed the obvious? With initials like that, the youngster was bound to invite ridicule and bullying. Perhaps it had been to ensure he was capable of handling the many hard knocks and bruises that were the invariable accompaniment to a tough life on the frontier. Doc liked to think so. It had certainly worked.

He took another sip of whiskey, savouring the warm glow as the effect bit deep.

The Mighty Atom!

Those were the days.

'Roll up, roll up! Welcome one and all to Doctor Jeremiah Spengler's Patent Travelling Medicine Show.'

He could almost hear the rich baritone of his father, the legendary proprietor, booming forth as he dextrously drew in the curious, the ailing and those who just enjoyed a good laugh. Life on the frontier could be dull and monotonous. Work, eat and sleep six days a week, and church twice on

Sundays. Any diversion was more than welcome.

Operating out of St Louis, Missouri, the purpose-built wagon travelled extensively between the small towns of the newly emergent frontier during the years immediately preceding the outbreak of the Civil War. The Medicine Show put on simple forms of entertainment for the crowd of which 'The Mighty Atom' became a well-loved favourite.

Primarily, the aim was to encourage the audience to part with their dollar-bills in exchange for an all-curative elixir. Doctor Spengler claimed that the secret recipe had been handed down through generations of medical experts and was the answer to almost every illness known to man. He would waft the bottle of black liquid tantalizingly in front of the gaping throng, eloquently reciting the prepared sales pitch.

'Ladies and gentlemen, I am exceedingly privileged to stand before you today and bring to your attention the most invigorating and universally acclaimed restorative ever likely to touch the lips of man.' Here a pause and a smile as he scanned the rapt audience before continuing: 'And ladies, of course. You are indeed the lucky ones, the chosen few. This preparation contains only the finest and rarest of ingredients to treat pains and strains, itches and twitches, congestion and indigestion, sneezes and wheezes, constipation and . . . flatulence.'

This latter announcement always received a hearty guffaw from the men, and haughty discomfiture from the ladies.

A brief pause to draw breath and he would resume the rousing diatribe with vigour.

'Yes indeed my friends, here can be found tonics and

tranquillizers, lotions and potions for the crippled or decrepit. Those of you suffering ills and chills will instantly be rejuvenated with my patented Elixir of Life. All for the bargain price of not five, not even three. Just one dollar will buy you the remedy for which you have been yearning.'

Doc couldn't help but smile at the recollection of his father's effervescent delivery.

It was at this point that the Doctor would take a moment to reflect. A pregnant silence held the gathering spellbound following his magniloquent oratory. Then he would point to a man of advancing years in the crowd.

'Are you married, sir?'

A bewildered nod from the selected watcher and Doctor Spengler would then proceed to profess avidly that the elixir prevented impotence in men of any age. One bottle and the recipient would be bounding about the bedchamber like a rampant lion.

The doctor would then sadly proclaim; 'Unfortunately, such is the popularity of this particular tonic that I am regrettably down to the last case.' This always witnessed a host of the more elderly gents in the crowd eagerly pushing forward.

Following a brief interlude, it would be Aaron's turn as 'The Mighty Atom'. This was to create the illusion that the show was an entertainment for the crowd's benefit and not merely a sales pitch for the variety of potions and ointments being hawked.

The Doctor would invite a brawny hulk of dubious intellect to climb on to the stage and try his hand at lifting a heavy set of bar-bells.

'You look a solid young fellow, hard-working and strong

I'll be bound,' he crowed, indicating an obvious candidate in the crowd. Few could resist the flattery to show off their bulging biceps. Spitting on palms and girding himself for the fray, the chosen guinea-pig would bend low, clutch the bar in its middle and take the strain, an arrogant smile being offered to less endowed watchers.

Then came the lift!

But nothing happened. The smile would disappear, the bewildered face assuming a deeply purple hue. Eyes bulged as blood pounded through the poor sap's head.

'We are waiting, my good sir,' intoned the Doctor, egging on the crowd. 'Surely such a feat is not beyond a Hercules such as yourself.'

Eventually, the fellow would be ignominiously forced to retire. Then it was the turn of 'The Mighty Atom.' Introducing Aaron as the strongest young Titan in the world, he would then ask his son to lift the weight.

Following a few muscle-flexing passes, the boy would lift the prodigious weight with ease, even holding it aloft with one hand. It was a magical exploit accomplished through deft sleight of hand. Aaron loved to see the hoards of ogling peepers as gasps of disbelief rippled through the assemblage. If only they had known how his father managed the trick. But nobody ever learned the truth.

Doc raised his rheumy eyes from the now empty glass. In the mirror behind the bar, a young man of twenty-five years going on forty stared back. The years since the Medicine Show disbanded had not been kind to the young gambler. His drawn features, the pallid, almost parchmentlike skin told of late nights huddled over winning and losing hands.

This was another of his father's areas of expertise that

Aaron had been taught from an early age. To such an extent that he could have cheated his way across the country had he so chosen without fear of discovery.

That was not Doc's way. Honesty, integrity and upholding the Spengler good name had originated from his mother's side of the family.

Elvira played her own unique role in the Medicine Show by claiming at the age of thirty-five to be entering her eightieth year. Naturally her flawless complexion was due in no small measure to a liberal consumption of Spengler's Vital Spark, the ultimate elixir of eternal youth. A birth certificate (genuine, of course) was indisputable evidence proving the veracity of such a claim.

But the years of constantly moving between towns, counties and even states took their toll. Everything was not always the easy-going life it might appear. Many was the time that a swift exit was judged prudent when Doctor Spengler's Patent Snake-Oil, Rattlesnake Liver Pills or Swamp-Root Balsam to name but a few samples, failed to produce the promised results. Angry pursuit and the painful consequences of retribution were a constant fear that went with the job.

Both father and son ought to have realized that a delicate creature like Elvira Spengler could not pursue such a life indefinitely without some untoward reaction. Aaron would never forget his twelfth birthday. That was also the day that cholera struck his mother down with devastating consequences.

The show was passing through the booming township of Denver, Colorado, during the spring of 1861 when Elvira Spengler finally breathed her last. She was buried in the cemetery on the edge of the old town two days later.

THREE

BUSHWHACKED

Watery eyes peered back from the bar-mirror as the years passed in front of him. It was the whiskey that always brought on these maudlin after-effects. Not so frequently these days. It was true what they said. Time does deaden the hurt. But it always remains, just below the surface waiting to jab at the conscience. Not that he could have done anything to prevent his mother's untimely demise. Cholera strikes without prejudice or discrimination. This truth was no salve to the feeling that he could have done something.

Blurred images reflected through the mirror, prodding at his addled brain – reminders that he was sorely in need of sleep. Slick Warriner and his chicanery was forgotten. Doc pushed himself off the bar, stuck the half-empty bottle in his pocket and headed for the door facing to Newton's main street.

The last vestiges of light were edging over the western horizon. Golden slivers faded to indigo as night took control. A dog barked in the distance. A faint scuffling beneath the boardwalk was followed by a choking squeal. Doc gave a knowing grunt. A feline predator was relishing its evening meal.

Head drooping on to his chest, he headed east towards the Palace Hotel, where he had a room. That direction led away from the bustling heart of the town. Street lighting was intermittent and all the shops and business premises were closed for the night. Doc gave it no thought. He stumbled onward, his blinkered thoughts only on seeking out his bed and getting a good night's sleep.

Others in the vicinity were more vigilant, intent on following the gambler's every move. It happened when he was mid-way between two dim oil-lamps. Three shadows struck, watched by a fourth. Without preamble they hustled the drink-sodden victim into a recessed corral heavy with the pitch of dark obscurity.

And there they set to work.

Doc was savagely flung to the ground.

Punching and kicking, the hired thugs were viciously egged on with the vengeful approval of their paymaster. Warriner hung back, allowing his underlings to do the business they knew best. Rip-snorting cattle towns like Newton always possessed their quota of riff-raff willing to do any kind of dirty work for a few bucks.

'Nobody gets away with pullin' the plug on Slick Warriner,' he snarled. The exposed card-sharp had obviously harboured a grudge that he intended following through to its bitter finale. His next remark was aimed at Magpie McGee.

'Use that lead cosh on him.'

The runt uttered a maniacal chortle. 'Clean forgot

about my little friend,' he cackled, eager to avenge his recent pistol-whipping.

Warriner joined in with a brutal toe-poke of his own.

Doc's floundering thoughts resolved into the obvious conclusion that Warriner must have found the little weasel in that room where he had been dumped. And now the varmint was after returning the favour. He cursed himself. How could he have been such a greenhorn. He ought to have realized that skunks of Warriner's ilk would seek painful revenge.

Too late for such misgivings now. With little success, he desperately tried to evade the flailing arms. Bunched fists, hard as rock, ploughed into his body. Each was propelled by a husky grunt.

Then a momentary pause brought him a grateful if brief respite from the punishing assault. The murky gloom, thick as pea-soup, was peeled back as the moon slid from behind a bank of cloud.

The paymaster's sickly grin twisted in alarm. Fearful that the ambush might be observed in the ghostly light, he rapped urgently; 'Get on with it, can't yuh. Somebody might come by at any moment.'

Dragging her valise behind her, Ginger LaPlage was cussing and hollering to herself. Maybe she should have let that little turd have a nibble, just to keep him quiet. It wouldn't have cost nothing and she'd still have been in work.

This wasn't the first time, and it damn sure wouldn't be the last. There was that slimy dude in Wichita who ran the Golden Globe theatre. Promised her the earth. And she would have fallen for his greasy charm if she had not seen him giving the same chat-up line to one of the chorus girls. A twinkling smile revealed snow-white teeth. That was one heck of a knee she had delivered to his vitals during their next tryst. Ginger laughed aloud. The poor guy had sure twitched and squirmed.

But that was the end of another good job. How much longer could she go on like this? Then her mind shifted to the bulging girth of Dandy Beau Merrick. A shiver ripped down the back of her Grecian neckline. The notion of that oil-rag and his smarmy ways almost made her throw up. Give in once and where would it end?

At that moment she tripped. Her high heel had stuck in a rabbit-hole. The valise flew one way, her perky green hat another. For some reason she kept hold of the parasol. Crawling around in the dark, red hair askew, stockings holed at the knee where she had fallen, Ginger felt as if her whole world was falling apart.

She nearly broke down. A wave of self-pity was about to wash over her. Another vehement oath against those responsible for her current plight passed her full lips.

That was when she noticed legs scuffling about on the far side of a fenced-off corral to her left. Boots flailing wildly. The six-foot high interlocking mesh of thin branches that enclosed the A2Z corral did not extend fully to ground level. A two-foot gap at the bottom had been left to allow bronc-busters a swift exit if thrown from their recalcitrant mounts.

This facility had allowed Ginger to witness a fracas that was most definitely one-sided.

'What was that?' hissed Warriner, his boot poised in mid-air.

'Eh?' This questioning gurgle from the Magpie.

'Thought I heard someone cussin'.'

'Likely just wind off the prairie.'

Riled up, rattled and ranting, Ginger recognized a fellow victim being persecuted. And in a brutish and painful manner too. She scrambled under the trellis and flung herself on the jasper who appeared to be directing the cowardly attack. Parasol waving like a battle flag at Gettysburg, she waded in, heedless of her own safety.

'You cowards be leaving that poor feller alone.'

Her furious holler was aimed at an evil-looking critter sporting a beige suit with maroon piping and a hat to match. Instantly she noted his eyes were too close together, cold and calculating. Taken by surprise, Warriner felt the parasol smack hard and solid against his jutting snout. A stream of blood piped from the injured appendage. He cried out in pain, backing off and stumbling over the writhing body of Doc Spengler.

Quickly coming round to appreciate the dire peril in which she had now placed herself, Ginger emitted a piercing scream fit to raise the Devil himself.

'Help! Murder!' she shrieked. Then, with a dash of temerity: 'Over here, Marshal. I've got 'em cornered.'

That was enough for the two hired bruisers. They immediately upped sticks and disappeared into the night.

'Let's be out of here, boss,' urged Magpie, tugging at Warriner who had scrambled unsteadily to his feet. 'We done what we came fer.'

'You gotten the lucre?' snapped Warriner.

'Sure thing.'

The card-sharp would have preferred a more terminal end to their bushwhacking foray. But even he realized that a rapid exit from the crime scene was called for.

Ginger emitted a deep sigh. Her breath gushed out in pulsating gasps.

'You OK, mister?'

The question was rather meaningless and she instantly regretted the utterance. He was obviously not all right. In fact he looked in a bad way. Blood dribbled from numerous cuts. But at least he was still conscious.

'Best we get you to a sawbones,' she said, struggling to lift the guy to his feet. Doc groaned as waves of nausea threatened to plunge him into the black pit of unconsciousness. Luckily, Ginger still had her purse slung round her neck. Delving inside, she produced a silver flask and unscrewed the top. 'Take a sip of this,' she offered. 'It'll fight back the sickness and calm your nerves.'

She tipped the brandy to his lips. He swallowed, coughing hard as the potent spirit burnt a path down his gullet.

'That do the trick?'

Doc nodded. The edge of darkness receded. He slumped against the corral fence trying to shrug off the lethargy. Another sip of brandy helped. Then he made a determined effort to focus on to this fiery vision that had saved him from being on the receiving end of a much worse beating, maybe even from losing his very life.

'No medic,' croaked Doc when his brain had returned to some semblance of normality. 'Just need some rest, that's all.' Doc's aversion to members of the medical fraternity stretched back to his youth, and his father's claim that they were all quacks. He still sustained the illusion. Even though he now knew that such notions were erroneous and it was the medicine shows that dispensed quackery, old habits died hard.

Ginger shrugged. 'Where you be staying then?'

'The Palace. Room 23, first floor.'

Placing an arm firmly around his waist, Ginger helped Doc take a tentative step. The heady aroma, a potent mix of roses and sweat, filtered out of the dishevelled tangle of red hair. Her hold was steady and firm, just like the body that now clung to him like a limpet. Not exactly an erotic gesture. But for the moment a welcome distraction from the multitude of aches and pains that pulsated from every facet of his own badly abused carcass.

Once inside his room, Doc tumbled on to the bed and was asleep in an instant. Ginger tugged off his boots and laid the heavily patched quilt over him. Soon the gentle murmur of sleep reminded the girl of her own fragile predicament.

' 'Tis all right for the likes of you, me fine feller,' she intoned, dabbing his bloodied face with a damp cloth. 'But what about the Good Fairy what saved yus?'

That was when she saw her reflection in the closet mirror.

'Holy Mother of Jesus!' The exclamation was one of pure shock and disbelief. Hands lifted to her blotched face and tangled locks, she tried to shut out the ghastly apparition that stared back at her. 'This is what you get for helping someone in a fix. And not a word of thanks did he offer.'

Not that she actually meant the disparaging comment. Her face creased in mock admonishment. Doc Spengler had been in no fit state to know anything that was happening. She peered down at his bruised features. Beneath the rapidly swelling nose, the black eye and the cut lip, he could almost be called handsome.

Dark curly hair hung down over a broad forehead. The

gaping mouth, discoloured and hanging loose, revealed pearly white teeth. It was a firm, solid face, dependable, one you could trust.

But that didn't help her situation at the present.

No way could she return to the Ramrod. For sure, that skunk Merrick would have passed the word to his bartenders to eject her if she showed up. And without funds, there was only one answer.

'Sorry, mister,' she muttered, half to herself whilst addressing the slumbering heap on the bed. 'I ain't got any choice.'

FOUR

UNFINISHED BUSINESS

It was almost noon when Doc finally surfaced. Spears of light beaming in through gaps in the drawn blinds played across his pallid features. A lethargic gurgle issued from the mashed face, simmering down to a throbbing grumble as sharpened nerve-ends bristled angrily. He raised himself on to one elbow and groaned aloud. Puffy eyes struggled to focus around pouches swollen to double their normal size. His mouth felt like a donkey's bum and tasted just as rank, the leathery tongue was rough with congealed blood.

He clawed his way off the bed and staggered over to the dresser. Outside a whip-crack split the air. His hand instinctively dropped to his hip. Then he realized: it was only another load of freight bound for the northern rail-head at Abilene.

He filled the wash-bowl and dunked his head in the

tepid water. A half-dozen quick swishes and out. Phew! That felt better. He still ached all over but at least his brain was clear. And Doc had learned from an early age that only with an active mind could a man tackle his problems.

That was when he saw her.

It had to be a woman, with a flaming head that curly. And all wrapped up in a quilt. His brown eyes popped behind the swelling. Then he remembered. The ambush, the beating, and the rescue. It was all rather hazy, a vague recollection. Somehow she must have got him up here and into his room. Thankfully she had left his clothes on the abused body.

He smiled. A warm, meaningful grin that elicited a pained yelp as torn and cracked lips parted. Tentatively he approached the slumbering creature. An arm reached out as he hovered over her supine form.

That was the moment Ginger chose to lift a mascara-smeared eyelash. What she witnessed produced a reflex jerk of her outstretched leg. Simultaneously, her left arm swung. Both of the crunching blows sent Doc ploughing backwards on to the bed. Ginger was on her feet in an instant, ready to fend off this blood-stained gargoyle. The writhing scowl faded to a jaw-dropping gawp as she remembered what had happened.

'What was that for?' complained Doc, rubbing his tender ear.

'You shouldn't ought to have come on me like that,' complained Ginger rather hesitantly. 'A girl has to protect herself in these lawless times.'

'It's not every day that a feller wakes up to find a fireball in his room, that's all.' He delved into a pocket of his torn jacket and removed a broken stogie, lit up and drew the smoke deep into his lungs. It was an instant palliative for his jangled nerves. 'Sorry if I scared you,' he added. The girl accepted the apology with a demure bob. 'Seems I owe you a debt of thanks.'

'I had nowhere else to stay. You won't throw me out, will you?' Ginger's emerald-green eyes lifted appealingly. It was her little-girl-lost look. It never failed to work.

'You saved my bacon last night Miss. . . ?'

'LaPlage, Ginger LaPlage,' she replied brightly. 'I'm the singer at the Crystal Theatre. Or was until that lecherous barrel of blubber, Beau Merrick, tried to have his evil way.' She gave an irate snort. 'Didn't take kindly to me refusing his advances so he cancelled my contract. And the bastard didn't even have the good grace to pay me what was owed.' Once again, her mouth turned in a provocative pout while she eyed Doc from beneath winged brows. 'You aren't for throwing me into the street, are you?'

Doc's stammered response was immediate.

'Of course not. After all you've done for me?' He paused, a thoughtful frown wrinkling his forehead. 'But we'll have to book you into a separate room. Us being single an' all.'

'Naturally,' agreed a smiling Ginger. Then she added hurriedly: 'I'll pay you back, mind. Soon as I get some work. Point is it won't be in this goddamned town. Merrick'll see to it that my name is blacklisted.'

Doc pondered on the dilemma.

'I'm about played out in this berg myself,' he said, lying back on the bed. 'How do you fancy Dodge City? They say it's red-hot now the railroad has arrived.'

She nodded eagerly.

'Soon as I'm on my feet, that is,' he added. A sudden twitch painfully reminded Doc that he was going nowhere for a few days until his body felt ready. He deliberately avoided mentioning that evening up the score with Slick Warriner was to be a priority before they left Newton.

'Don't worry yourself,' fussed Ginger, straightening her dishevelled clothing and realizing what a sight she must look. 'I'll tend to your every need. Within reason of course.' Her perky nose lifted coyly.

'Of course,' echoed the smirking gambler.

'So what do I call you?'

'They call me Doc Spengler.'

'You a regular sawbones then?'

'Not exactly,' replied Doc somewhat cautiously. 'It's a long story. I'll tell you later.'

'Suit yourself.' Ginger shrugged, then flounced over to the mirror to repair her painted face.

It was in fact a week before Doc felt able to venture out of the hotel. In that time, Ginger had brought his meals and tended to his injuries. Due to her timely intervention, no serious damage had been done.

Unfortunately their time was running out. On two occasions the manager of the hotel had paid him a visit concerning the outstanding account for his protracted stay. Doc had assured him that payment was no problem and he would be reimbursed in the next few days, before they checked out.

Truth of the matter was, he was broke. Warriner might have been stymied regarding the intended retribution for being branded a cheat, but he had made sure to relieve the bushwhacked victim of his winnings. Luckily, Doc always kept an emergency fund in a concealed pocket of his jacket.

That was almost gone. It had paid for his and Ginger's food together with some bandages and salves for his injuries. The rest had bought some much-needed duds from a used-clothing warehouse.

He emptied his pockets on to the bed.

'Fifteen dollars and twenty cents,' he sighed.

'What we be going to do then, me fine bucko?' Ginger's light banter failed to control the sense of panic in her lyrical tone.

Doc considered. His brow crinkled like a ploughed field. This was not the first time he had been without funds. Doubtless it wouldn't be the last. He stood fastening his black necktie. Ginger had lit the oil-lamps. Outside, dark shadows veiled the clapboard false-fronts along Drover's Alley. Fading splashes of iridescent flame sunk beneath the western horizon. There was only one course open to them.

The Palace Hotel was going to have to whistle for its bill.

'Pack your things and bring them in here. Make sure nobody sees you.'

She offered him a quizzical frown. 'What gives?' she asked.

'We're moving out. And only pack the essentials. We're travelling light.' The tone was snapped off, raw and edgy. Its brittle nature made her take a step back.

This was a new side to Doc Spengler. The tough organizer, brusque and ruthless when the occasion demanded. And this was just such an occasion.

He handed Ginger a ten-dollar bill.

'Book us on to the night stage in the names of Mr and Mrs . . . Smith. It leaves at ten sharp.' He studied a silver-plated pocket watch boasting pictures of his mother and father. The time read 8.15 p.m. His face assumed a dark, obscure look. The deep-set eyes were cold and flinty. A distant, almost blank expression overlaid his drawn features. 'While you're out, there are a couple of things that need attending to. I'll meet you at the depot.'

She didn't pose any query this time. Instead she gave a curt nod and left.

At 8.30 Doc slid up the sash-window and peered out into the darkness. His room was at the rear of the hotel, backing on to an alley. It was a feature he always opted for with just such an eventuality in mind. He threw the two carpetbags down, then fed out a rope fashioned from the bed sheets. Another quick glance to right and left and he was shinning down the makeshift escape route.

At this hour the alley was dark and silent. Doc tensed as he landed softly, nerves strung tight as a banjo. He retrieved the bags, and headed uptown.

His first visit was to the Crystal Theatre.

Leaving the bags under the raised ground-level flooring, he located a set of steps at the back leading up to the first floor. Ginger had told him all about the Crystal and its lay-out. Not that she'd had any inkling of what his intentions were. He slipped through into a corridor and quickly padded along to a door labelled *Manager – Beau Merrick Esquire.*

Ear jammed against the door, he listened intently. From inside the room a stilted whistling sorted itself into a popular song of the day. Merrick appeared to be in good spirits. He would soon be laughing on the other side of his face. Doc's lips drew back into a mirthless smile as turned the door-handle, the Remington palmed and ready.

Merrick was seated behind a large desk. He struck Doc as resembling a corpulent toad, the wide, fleshy mouth bounded by thin shiny lips. He was counting a stack of greenbacks, clearly the early night's takings.

He looked up, piggy eyes suspicious but revealing a hint of fear.

'What do you want?' he stammered, awkwardly shuffling the heap of notes together. 'This is a private area not open to the public.'

'That's all right,' answered Doc easily, bringing the six-shooter from behind his back. 'It's private business that I want to discuss.' He turned abruptly and locked the door. 'We don't want to be disturbed now, do we?'

'W-what business do you have with me?' Merrick's round eyes fastened on to the level, unwavering shooter.

'It's about some wages you owe to a friend of mine.'

'Who might that be?' When it seemed that he was not about to be gunned down on the spot, or robbed, Merrick assumed some of his previous bluster. 'As far as I am aware, all wages have been paid out.'

'Not to Ginger LaPlage they haven't.'

The manager froze. His puffy cheeks flushed. A guilty conscience or fear? He had to think quickly.

'Well?'

'The reasons for Miss LaPlage being dismissed are private and confidential. She walked out on the show thus breaking her contract.' Merrick felt on safe ground here. There was no proof of any misdemeanour that would hold up in a court of law. It was his word against hers. 'She forfeited all money due to her.'

'Well, I'm claiming it on her behalf,' rasped Doc acidly. He took a step towards the flabby bloater and grabbed a pile of notes from the desk counting off forty dollars. 'That's for four nights performing in this flea-pit. And another one hundred for my collection fee. Plus an extra fifty for expenses.' He peeled off the stated amount and flung the rest at the fuming manager.

Purple veins stood proud like wriggling worms on Merrick's neck. He looked ready to bust wide open.

'That's daylight robbery,' he raged.

'I'd call it night-time compensation,' smirked Doc, pocketing the dough. 'Now get your clothes off.'

'What?'

'You heard. I won't tell you a second time.' The threatening pistol, now cocked and wagging in a hostile fashion, discouraged the manager's refusal to co-operate. 'And make it fast. I ain't got time to argue.' He jammed the hard steel of the weapon brutally into Merrick's stomach.

The toad yelped but complied, quickly divesting himself of his garments down to a bright-red pair of briefs. Doc couldn't help but chuckle at the sight.

'Now turn around,' he hissed, withdrawing a hank of rope from his jacket. Expertly he secured the dude's hands and feet, quickly stifling the belligerent protests with a necker across his mouth. He was now ready to add the icing to the cake, the *pièce de résistance* of his plan.

Doc slipped the loose end of the rope fastening Merrick's feet over an exposed ceiling beam, took a firm grip, then heaved. The burbling porker was no feather-duster. And Doc had only recently recovered from a severe beating. Blood pumped in his head. It took every morsel of concentrated power to achieve this final slap in the kisser for the odious heap of dung. Slowly the writhing burden lifted a few inches clear of the carpeted office floor. Then he tied the rope down to the heavy desk.

Short panting gasps had taken their toll. But through the ruddy features, a leery grin told of a job well done. He raised a boot and pushed the twirling body. Muffled croaks issued from behind the tight necker. Merrick's eyes flicked about in terror, praying that somehow the humiliating nightmare would resolve itself.

'Time for me to depart, Mister Merrick,' sniggered Doc, further agitating the swaying dandy with his boot. He wagged an admonitory finger in front of the blubbering toady, whispering: 'And when someone finally cuts you down, you would be well advised not to follow me south to Wichita.'

Doc raised his hat and offered an exaggerated bow. Then he was gone.

Before joining his travelling-companion at the stage depot he had one more call to make. Keeping to the shadows as much as possible, he made his silent way along to the Ramrod saloon. Boisterous laughter mingling with a noise that might vaguely be termed music emanated from the crowded interior. Inside were the usual array of pasteboard-pushers and drinkers.

Doc peered over the slatted batwing doors. No sign of Slick Warriner. Careful to avoid attention, he slipped inside, tugging his hat-brim down to obscure his features. A last look round, then he sidled over to the bar and ordered a small beer.

'Slick Warriner running a game tonight?' he casually asked the bartender whilst sipping his drink.

'Not tonight, or any other night,' came back the blunt reply.

'How come?'

'He was caught cheating. The boss told him to sling his hook.' The barkeep sniffed, his bulbous snout twitching with false rebuke. Like all beer-pullers, he knew everything that occurred under his own roof. And probably resented having his rake-off terminated. 'We don't cotton to card-sharps in this establishment.'

Doc suppressed an acerbic retort.

'Who runs this place then?'

The barman eyed him suspiciously. 'You ask an awful lot of questions, mister.'

'Just interested is all,' he countered, sinking into a drinker's slouch.

Big Nose snorted, then provided the required answer.

'If you must know it's Dandy Beau Merrick, the manager over at the Crystal Theatre, who owns the Ramrod.' He stood squarely in front of the questioner, hands on broad hips. Then gave a waspish snap. 'Anything else?'

Doc ignored the jibe. His blank poker-face betrayed none of the anger bubbling inside. Merrick again. He might have known. He glanced down at his watch.

9.56 p.m.

He tipped the glass to his lips, and finished the drink. Then turned and made a purposefully slow exit. The barkeep's piercing gaze pursued him out of the saloon. Once outside, Doc scurried along to the depot.

FIVE

DODGE CITY

The night stage was ready. Driver and guard were perched up front ready to whip the team of six into motion. The passengers were at that moment ready to embark. Luggage had been secured on the roof of the stagecoach and the mail clerk was checking the inventory. Satisfied with the tally, he handed the leather bags up to the driver who stowed them in the boot beneath his seat.

Doc gave a nod of approval. It was one of the latest Concord Specials. Only once before had he ridden one of the superbly crafted vehicles. That was on the Butterfield run from St Louis to Denver back in 1869, the year of that legendary merging of the cross-continental railway at Promontory Point in Utah. Now that would have been one epic moment to have witnessed. Sam Montague of the Canadian Pacific shaking hands with Grenville Dodge.

And it was the town to which the Union Pacific chairman had given his name that he and Ginger LaPlage were now headed.

42

Dodge City.

'You just admirin' the view or catchin' the stage, mister?'

Doc was jerked from his reverie by the driver. Whipcrack Larson was a grizzled veteran of many stage runs whose thick grey moustache and beard completely obscured a wind-blasted visage. Not to mention a half-dozen arrow scars from Indian attacks. He was proud of the fact that none of the coaches under his control had ever been lost. Or been late arriving. And he was not about to endanger that record tonight. The equine team recognized their boss's irritation and in consequence were equally anxious to hit the trail.

'Has my companion arrived yet?' asked Doc, unaware that anything was amiss.

'And who might that be?' growled the fractious driver, anxious to get his plaited snake cracking.

At that moment Ginger stuck her head out of the coach window.

'Thank goodness you've arrived,' she panted, straightening a perky little hat atop the blazing inferno. 'Where have you been? The driver was all for pulling out.'

Larson interrupted, snapping his long whip meaningfully.

'Cut the jawin' and climb aboard,' he grumbled, 'I'm already three minutes late.'

In the time it takes to skin a flea, the bouncing Concord was rumbling down Drover's Alley heading west. Soon the jumping cacophony of Newton was left behind as the six passengers settled down for the night run to Abbyville where the horses would be changed. It was a direct run across the flat prairie land and the team easily settled into a measured regularity.

Streaks of gold faded to purple as the night shift took over. Hawks cawed to each other. Prairie-owls hooted. In the distance a coyote howled its sad lament to the moon. The rhythmic jolting quickly lulled the passengers into a somnolent doze. Only Doc remained awake. He had much to absorb his mind, not least the itchy thought that Slick Warriner was likewise bound for Dodge City. No proof. Just a niggling hunch, and the barkeep's too trite assertion that he had headed south.

Crossing his arms, he casually surveyed his fellow-travellers.

Opposite, a portly dude sat with his good lady, heading for a new life in the rapidly expanding township. The dark suit and clean-cut image was a sure sign of the successful banker. And a town like Dodge City would require at least two such financial establishments these days. Then there was the soldier-boy, clearly heading for Fort Dodge. And, judging by his pristine uniform, a recently graduated officer. Lastly, and most intriguing, was a guy in his mid-thirties clad in a thigh-length buckskin jacket, worn but serviceable. Just like the pearl-handled revolver on his hip.

Doc frowned. Cattle buyer? Ranch foreman? Or maybe a new lawdog. From its inception following the Civil War, Dodge had certainly acquired a mean reputation for lawlessness and gun-slinging on a grandiose scale. The military had no jurisdiction over the town and any law enforcement that did exist was in its infancy.

Perhaps this guy was one of those new 'town-tamers' Doc had heard about. He gave the slumbering traveller a keen-eyed appraisal. Especially the gleaming six-shooter. The word was that law officers were being issued with a new and much more reliable firearm than the old cap-'n-ball loaders. Produced by Sam Colt's company, in only a few months they had been labelled the Peacemaker.

Doc's interest was aroused. He promised himself in the morning to find out more regarding this new handgun. Perhaps they were now on general issue and he could acquire one as well.

Another ten minutes and even Doc Spengler had succumbed to the soporific effect of the drumming hoofs and swaying carriage.

Next thing he knew, the driver was calling out that they were approaching Abbyville and an hour's stop over. There would be the chance to get some breakfast, and stretch out stiff and aching muscles. The padded seats might be comfortable, but after eight hours of constant jolting even the most resilient posterior was apt to scream in protest. A break was welcomed by all.

Over a breakfast of fried bacon, beans and corn dodgers, Doc prodded the mysterious stranger for information.

'You headin' for Dodge then?' he enquired, sipping at the tin mug of coffee.

'Yep.'

'On business?'

'Could be.'

This critter wasn't giving anything away. Sitting next to a surly conversationalist of this ilk, the rest of the journey was going to be one huge barrel of laughs. Still Doc persisted.

'They tell me Dodge is one rip-snorting berg where anything goes.' He glanced askance at the stranger's raw-boned features, the long blond hair and drooping moustache. He was hoping for some reaction, and in this he was not disappointed.

'Not fer long,' came back the acidic rejoinder.

Ah! So he had been right all along. This guy had to be the new marshal. 'You the new law then?'

The man's powder-blue eyes drilled right through him, cold and detached. Without another word, he stood and left the way station, leaving Doc nonplussed.

Resenting the rather brusque affront, he called after the tall man's retreating back.

'You gotten a handle, mister lawman?'

Pausing in the doorway, the man turned and surveyed the room. His buckskin-fringed jacket flapped in the morning breeze, playing hide-and-seek with the enigmatic Colt. Beneath the broad-brimmed hat, a keen scrutiny arrowed the speaker.

'Calloway,' he said, almost in a whisper. 'R.S. Calloway.'

A gasp issued from pursed lips.

Buckskin Bob!

Everybody west of the Missouri knew Robert Stanford Calloway. If not personally, then certainly by reputation. The guy was a legend. And a merciless killer.

Doc's ruddy face broke out in a cold sweat. He knew now that the man's new hogleg was most definitely not for show. The rowdy elements that frequented Dodge City's infamous Front Street were in for an alarming shock. And as a member of the gambling fraternity, Doc would need to watch his own precarious situation.

Having absorbed the startling news that they were travelling with the infamous Buckskin Bob Calloway, the journey continued with no further revelations. The stagecoach gradually ate up the miles across the undistinguished grassland, featureless except for the hundreds of buffalo corpses that littered the vast prairie.

Ginger curled her lip at the nauseating vision from hell. Survival on the frontier meant displaying a tough resilient exterior to the world at large. But inside, she was still a woman. Brutality and blood-lust just for the sake of procuring animal skins made her stomach lurch.

Doc took no heed of his companion's discomfort. His thoughts were wholly absorbed by their infamous fellow passenger. He eventually drummed up the courage to ask the marshal about his new gun. Calloway was more than willing to extol the virtues of the .45's efficient action and rapid loading, using the new self-contained cartridges. He even allowed Doc to examine it.

The most important disclosure of all confirmed that the gun was now on general release. And he was assured that Dodge City gunsmiths would certainly have received their stock by now.

'Won't be no use to yuh,' voiced Calloway firmly, shaking his head.

Doc gave him a sidelong glance.

'I intend applying to the town council for an ordinance banning all handguns within the city limits.'

Three days after leaving Newton the stagecoach made its final approach to Dodge City. The trail passed between huge stock-pens crammed with thousands of steers awaiting shipment to the hungry cities of the East. The pulsating hum of lowing cattle filled the air, a sad and forlorn dirge as if they realized this was truly the end of the line for them.

Then they were through, entering the broad thoroughfare of Front Street. On either side, smart false-fronted buildings intermingled with tents and shacks. As yet there were no permanent structures of solid brick. The rail tracks of the Atchison, Topeka and Santa Fe ran down the middle, dividing the street into two separate sectors.

On the north side stacks of buffalo hides littered the street. Piled higher than the stagecoach, they were under the supervision of grizzled hunters. The odour was appalling. It permeated their very being.

The banker's wife had to be given smelling-salts to prevent her from fainting. Beside her, eyes bulging and mouth hung askew, her husband wondered what sort of hell's kitchen he had chosen to make his new home. The army captain's attempt to affect a knowing demeanour failed dismally. Coughing and spluttering, Ginger dabbed a scented handerchief to her aquiline nose throughout the ordeal. Doc was too entranced by the potential earnings offered by such a rampant cesspit to be bothered by any irritant like a bad smell. Dollar signs flashed before his eyes.

Only Buckskin Bob remained unaffected, casually puffing on a cheroot.

The stage drew to a halt outside the depot.

'Dodge City!' announced Whipcrack Larson, dragging on the leathers and stamping hard on the brake-lever. 'End of the line. Anybody needs a hotel and eating-house, I can heartily recommend the Great Western. Softest beds, smartest rooms, and the best steaks in Kansas.'

Doc smiled to himself, surmising that the old-timer had done this many times before. He idly wondered whether Larson received a back-hander for every passenger who took up the offer. Good luck to him if he did.

'No company in the beds I trust?' Doc's mouth creased in a wry curl.

Larson gave the speaker an indignant scowl. 'Not so much as a flea, bug or roach anywhere in the place. Ma Clementine runs a clean establishment. If'n she heared what you was a-sayin', mister, she'd have your guts fer garters.'

'Just asking, is all,' muttered Doc, collecting his carpetbag. Then he headed in the direction indicated by the testy driver.

'What about me then?' called Ginger, struggling with her valise.

Doc paused in mid-stride, then turned. He figured his obligation for the lady's timely assistance back in Newton had been paid out in full. Now she was on her own. He was about to mumble some platitude to that effect when a deep baritone intervened.

'Allow me, ma'am.' It was Buckskin Bob. He hefted the valise on to his broad shoulders and took hold of her bag before strolling past a shamefaced Doc Spengler. 'I am acquainted with the owner,' he said, 'and will see to it you are given the best room in the hotel.'

'Well, thank you kindly, sir.' She smirked, arrogantly strutting past Doc, her pert nose sniffing derisively. 'It is pleasing to note there are still some gentlemen around these days.'

Doc awkwardly followed them like a lapdog, pursued by a yarraping guffaw from Whipcrack Larson.

'That little gal's sure gotten your measure, feller,' he chuckled.

Having signed in at the Great Western, Doc wasted no time. He needed a quick win to resurrect his dicey fortunes. He had a small grubstake, courtesy of Beau Merrick. But what he really needed was a decent run of luck at the tables.

His hand dropped to the Remington on his hip. A good enough handgun in its day. Although he'd had it so long that the worn mechanism was making the action rather sloppy. Someday, maybe soon, it was going to jam at the wrong moment. What he really needed was one of those Colt Peacemakers – nickel-plated with his initials carved on to an ivory butt.

A wistful look flitted across the pale visage as raised voices dragged his thoughts back to the matter in hand. Momentarily stopping in front of an open door, he scanned the interior of the saloon.

Suddenly, the blast of gunfire assailed his lugs. A small man staggered backwards through the batwings, clutching his shoulder, a rapidly expanding smear of red staining the blue denim shirt. Another man quickly followed. This second guy was large and rotund but quick on his feet. He was a brutish-looking rannie sporting a black beard. But most distinctive was a black patch over his left eye. The peaked cap identified him as a seafarer.

A vague idea that he had met this hustler before pricked at Doc Spengler's mind. It hailed from way back in the distant mists of time. He scratched at his thick side-whiskers. A puzzled frown played across the lined fore-head as he stood back, a curious spectator to this violent pantomime being enacted before him.

Patch threw a heap of pasteboards at the twitching body lying in the muddy street.

'Nobody accuses Clipper Jim Tandy of cheating without good cause,' he snarled, waving his shooter around. It was a diminutive Remington Number 2 pocket revolver, but no less effective for that. 'You come into the Long Branch again and I'll bury you myself on Boot Hill.' This was a reference to the recently opened cemetery on the edge of town. Already it had become the final resting-place of numerous gunslingers and outlaws. The speaker swung on his heel growling, 'Will somebody get this chiseller to a medic?'

The plugged man groaned but managed to clamber to his feet. Drawing his own gun he hauled back the hammer and aimed at the retreating figure of Clipper Jim.

A shot rang out. But not from the injured critter's hogleg.

The little man spun like a dervish and crashed on to the boardwalk. This time he lay still, unmoving.

A voice that Doc had come to recognize all too well split the ether.

'Backshooters don't deserve the attentions of a sawbones. Card-sharps neither.' The smoking Colt of Buckskin Bob Calloway twirled on its owner's finger before disappearing into the well-oiled holster. He slowly mounted the boardwalk and walked right past Doc up to Clipper Jim.

Calloway held the other with a tight, even regard.

'Nor do I want any shooting in *my* town other than from my gun. You gotten a grievance, then my office door is always open.'

The nautical gambler's eyes, shifty and loose, betrayed a wariness and a cautious respect for this doughty representative of the law.

'Understand, mister?' rasped Calloway pointedly.

'S-sure thing, Marshal,' stammered Tandy, backing

away. The marshal's reputation had clearly spread far beyond the central plains. 'Anything you say.'

'It's the undertaker that's needed here, not a doctor,' Calloway finished before continuing on his way as if nothing had happened. As if on cue, a tall skeletal figure in black appeared with a tape-measure.

Doc licked his dry lips, guarded eyes probing the marshal's retreating back. The guy had just killed a human being as if he were snuffing out a candle. With not a flicker of emotion. The cold hand of the grim reaper caressed Doc's spine, reminding him to be extra cautious during his sojourn in Dodge City.

Inside the Long Branch, Clipper Jim Tandy had resumed his seat and was opening a new deck of cards. There was now a free chair. Doc found himself pushing through the crowd to join the game. He felt inexorably drawn to this odd character. He knew him from somewhere. But where?

'You in or out?' The gruff bark accompanied by a dispassionate stare was made all the more cutting by the lone peeper. Like a black chunk of coal, it bored into the newcomer.

Doc pulled back a chair, ignoring the gambler's ploy to unsettle his opponents. Reaching into his pocket, he brought out a hefty roll of banknotes – the 'inconvenience fee' extracted from Dandy Beau Merrick. A wry smile cracked his taciturn demeanour at the recollection of Merrick 'hanging around', waiting to be rescued.

Tandy shuffled the cards and pushed them to the player on his right to be cut.

The atmosphere in the saloon was oppressive. Smoke hung in the stagnant air, the lurid glow from numerous oil-lamps creating a mesmeric effect. Tandy dabbed at his sweating brow. His ruddy seaman's complexion, shiny and damp, was more used to the open decks of sailing-ships.

'Too damned hot in this oven,' he grunted, shrugging out of a blue jerkin. 'Give me a life on the ocean waves any day.' Then he rolled up the sleeves of his shirt to reveal knotted arms heavily muscled from hauling thick ropes.

But it was the tattoo etched into the skin of the forearm that caught Doc's steady gaze. His whole body tensed, eyes narrowing to thin slits. His hands clutched at the table edge, the knuckles white as ivory.

The skull and crossbones!

Now he knew exactly where he had seen this jasper before.

SIX

FALSE ACCUSATION

It was the raised voice that attracted young Aaron Spengler's attention. A harsh guttural outpouring that seemed to originate from the caravan interior where his father was counting up the day's takings. Aaron had been repairing his Mighty Atom outfit ready for the next performance when the bitter argument broke his concentration.

And it was no mere bandying of words. No minor altercation. Inside the caravan was a very angry man clearly bent on retribution for some perceived felony on Doctor Jeremiah's part.

Disgruntled customers were not a new phenomenon to the Medicine Show. Those who persisted with their complaints, or threatened to call in the forces of law and order if they existed, could usually be placated with a refund plus a little extra as compensation. On occasion, the caravan and its retinue had been forced to make a hasty departure when Doctor Jeremiah's unctuous charm had failed to smooth the troubled waters.

This tirade sounded much more serious.

Aaron crept closer to the short flight of steps leading up into the body of the caravan. His father was desperately trying to mollify ruffled feathers. To Aaron's straining ears he did not appear to be succeeding in this endeavour.

'It was snake-oil you bought,' insisted a quaking Jeremiah Spengler. 'That stuff is for rubbing into the affected part of the body to ease pain. It sure ain't for drinking.'

'You oughta have told me that when I bought it,' railed the irate punter, hammering a mallet-like fist down on to the table. 'My wife's gone and died on me 'cos of what you been a-peddlin'.'

'I am most distressed that your good lady has passed away. But you should have read the instructions on the bottle.' Here the Doctor picked up a sample and pointed to the all-important wording. He read it out slowly. 'Not for internal use.' There it was, emblazoned in bold type. 'How can you hold me responsible for this unfortunate accident if you choose to ignore the instructions.'

'Accident?' ranted the man, grabbing the offending bottle and hurling it against the wall. 'You murdered that woman with your goddanmed poison. I didn't read the blasted thing 'cos ... well ...' Here he paused as the depth of emotion gushed out in a spluttering response. 'I can't flamin' well read. You should have told me.' Tears of frustration were suddenly replaced by a steely glint in his eyes, icy and manic. 'Now I'm gonna see to it that nobody else goes the same way as my Elsa.'

Jeremiah's voice cracked with panic. 'W-what do you m-mean?' he stuttered.

The hairs on Aaron's neck bristled as he heard that dreaded click: the double snap that could only come from a revolver being hauled back to full cock ready for firing. He wanted to dash up the steps and help his father. It wasn't his pa's fault that someone had died. The guy should have been more careful.

But Aaron's feet were made of lead. Stunned, unable to move, he cowered beneath the steps, waiting for the blast of gunfire. Fear, panic, shock. All combined to ensure that Aaron Spengler remained glued to the floor, unable – or was it unwilling – to intervene. It had haunted his dreams ever since.

Could he have saved his father's life?

Not even the two sharp reports galvanized him into action.

A choking cry that disintegrated to an anguished gurgle told him the awful threat had been no mere act of bravado. Bottles shattered as Jeremiah slammed back against the thin walls of the caravan.

A brief silence followed. Somewhere in the distance a dog barked. Then heavy boots stamped towards the door and down the steps. Aaron stayed where he was, thankfully concealed in the murky shadows. Mouth dry, throat parched, Aaron held his breath, not daring to move a muscle. The killer stopped at the bottom, turned and looked back towards the open door. The boy cowered back, seeking to merge with the shadows, terrified of being spotted.

That hesitation on the killer's part was enough. Aaron's thin frame may have been frozen into rigid immobility. But his eyes betrayed no hesitation in picking out every detail of this murdering skunk. Standing barely six feet from where Aaron was hiding, the man stood framed in the afternoon sunlight, a perfect if gruesome vision. Over the right eye – a black patch, the sailor's peaked cap, and a tattoo on the left forearm. Faded with age, it looked like a grinning skull with a pair of crossed bones beneath – the symbol of the Jolly Roger displayed by pirate ships of old. And in his left hand, an old cap-and-ball Navy Colt, smoke drifting from the barrel.

The man uttered a stifled grunt. Then he was gone.

But that picture was seared on Aaron's brain. He could not recall the killer's face, age or what he was wearing. But he had seen enough. Someday he would find the seaman with the black patch and tattoo – and take full and due reprisal for his father's brutal slaying.

That was a promise he now intended to keep.

'It'll cost you twenty bucks to see my hand.' The retort, forced and brittle, was intended to bluff his opponent into thinking he had an unbeatable hand. The probing eye beneath the peaked cap was cool, impassive. Not a muscle twitched on the weathered countenance as he waited.

Doc's gaze fell to the cards he was tightly clutching. Instead of the diamond straight, all he saw was blood pumping from the fatal wounds in his father's chest. His watery eyes glazed over, the overheated room fading to a dull haze as obscure images flitted across his blurred vision. And in the centre a dark shadow, the killer whom he had been seeking all these years.

Slowly, as if resolving from a dream, the apparition in Doc's memory began to take earthly shape, the edges sharpening as clarity returned with a vengeance. And there he was, on the other side of the table.

His father's killer.

A series of reflexes clicked into place. Years of constantly programming his mind to react in a certain way meant there was no going back now. Doc's instincts were operating to a prearranged pattern separate from his brain. The response was automatic.

There was no venting of anger. No demonic howling for retribution. The only sign of human sentiment was the blood draining from his face, leaving a blanched, icy mask. Burning watchful eyes pierced the yellow fog that hung suspended beneath the ceiling timbers of the bar-room as they fastened on to the object of his hate.

As if in slow motion, the young man stood, at the same time drawing the Remington in a single fluid motion. The barrel rose, his thumb wound back the hammer, his forefinger squeezing the trigger. The final denouement had arrived.

Then.

A blinding display of coloured lights exploded inside his head. From far away subliminal impulses in his brain teetered on the edge of a deep abyss before plunging him headlong into a pit of blackness.

Opening his eyes, Doc found himself staring at a brick wall. Beams of light filtered through a small barred window playfully poking at the dust motes floating in the air. He clamped a hand to his temple, trying to ease the throbbing in his head. A pained wince issued from pursed lips as his fingers contacted a huge lump swathed in bandages.

He groaned aloud. Reality had returned with a vengeance.

This had to be the Dodge City hoosegow. And that bastard Calloway had slugged him from behind. Recollection of that fateful meeting in the Long Branch came flooding back. He'd had the guy in his sights. And Calloway had ruined it for him. He was in jail and the killer was still on the loose.

Real anger surged to the fore.

'You goddamed son-of-a-bitch, Calloway,' he yelled, grabbing the bars of the cell door. A spear of agony hammered inside his skull. 'Pistol-whipping me just as I had that killer dead in my sights. Let me outa here!' He rattled the bars impotently. There was no chance of escaping his incarceration. But at least it helped to curb his frustration.

The door from the outer office opened.

'Finally surfaced, have yuh?' Buckskin Bob filled the entrance, a mug of coffee in his hand. His elongated shadow spread along the dirt floor of the cell block passage. The knee-length buckskin coat gave him the appearance of a mountain trapper. 'And keep that noise down, mister. Else you ain't gettin' no breakfast.' He took a measured sip of the potent brew. 'This sure is good Java. And I gotten some chow out here. There's too much for me and it'd be a pure waste feeding it to the pigs.'

The smell wafted through the gap making Doc realize how hungry he was. That thought made him simmer down. It also helped stifle the rank odour of unwashed blankets and the slop bucket festering in a corner of the cell.

'How long I been in here?' he asked.

'Couple a days.'

'Did you have to slug me so hard,' grumbled Doc, tentatively feeling the lump.

'I told you before. Any shootin' in this town would be of my makin',' explained Buckskin Bob. 'And with you aimin' to blow that dude's head off . . .' He clicked his tongue while shrugging his broad shoulders and leaving the rest unsaid.

'But I had just cause,' countered Doc with vigour.

'How d'yuh figure that then?'

A meaningful pause followed.

'He gunned down my pa in cold blood.' Doc's low pronouncement held the marshal with a challenging resonance. 'Seems to me like that's cause enough for any man to draw his gun and set to shooting.'

'Not on my patch it ain't. I need proof. And then it'll be a judge and jury that decides the outcome. Not some gun-happy card-sharp.' Calloway arrowed the younger man with a withering glare. 'There'll be no vigilante law in my town.' Then his face softened into a wry smile. 'You ready for some grub now?'

Doc realized that the lawman was right. But he still resented the marshal's painful interference, not to mention the insinuation that he was a double-dealer.

He nodded. 'I could eat a two-inch prime rib with fried potatoes and all the trimmings.'

'You'll get bacon and beans and like it,' scoffed Calloway, retreating to the outer office.

It was some two hours later when Calloway returned in the company of the alleged killer. Leaving Clipper Jim in the outer office, he opened the cell block door and came through. He lounged idly against the wall opposite the barred door. Doc lay sprawled out on the hard palliasse, hands behind his head, staring up at the rough-cast adobe ceiling.

'The fella what gunned down yer pa,' began the marshal evenly. 'Which eye did you say was covered by a black patch?'

Doc's gaze remained fixed on a crack in the ceiling.

'The right eye.'

'Uhmmm!' murmured Calloway nodding. 'And which hand was holding the gun?'

Doc shifted his gaze over to the marshal, a puzzled frown puckering his brow.

'Why the interrogation, marshal?'

'Just answer the questions, mister. The right, or the left?'

Doc had no hesitation in saying it was the left hand.

Buckskin arrowed him with a dour look, his thin lips drawn back into a caustic smile.

'Just one more thing,' he rasped harshly. 'This tattoo. Which arm did you say? Think hard on what you're a-sayin'.'

Doc sat up. A chilly ripple of trepidation fingered his spine. What was this guy about? Why all the quizzing?

'There ain't no doubt,' snapped Doc, emphatically slamming his balled fist into the straw mattress. 'No doubt. at all. The tattoo was on the bastard's left arm, he was a left-handed gunman, and the right eye, face on, had a patch.'

The marshal gave a curt nod, then called to someone in the outer office.

'You can come through now, Captain Tandy.'

The gambler from the Long Branch entered the passage and joined Calloway in front of Doc's cell.

'Now take a good look at this feller,' said the marshal, addressing his prisoner, 'and tell me what you see.'

Doc's mouth gaped wide. He was stunned to silence.

'I'll tell you what you see,' continued Calloway pointing to each item in turn. 'A patch over the . . . left eye. A tattoo on the . . . right arm. And a shooter on the right hip.' He stared hard at Doc. Bob was living up to his reputation. His harsh tone rose to a throaty rasp. 'Not a single one right. Now what you gotta say? Is this the man that killed your pa?' He grabbed the bars. 'Well, is it?'

Doc was stunned into a blunt silence.

'Maybe I did make a mistake,' he answered eventually in a subdued voice. 'Anyone could do that after twelve years.'

'If I hadn't been on hand,' snapped Calloway, 'an inno-cent man would have been killed. And you'd have been up on a murder rap.'

Doc turned to the sailor. 'What can I say, mister. You had all the makings.'

'But all in the wrong positions,' growled the burly sailor. His frosty tone and brutal regard indicated he would have liked nothing more than to string the young prisoner up from the highest yard-arm of one of his ships. 'You'd be well advised to keep outa my way in future.' With that brittle warning, he swung on his heel.

'There won't be any need for you to avoid Captain Tandy,' added Calloway with a biting inflection after the sailor had left.

'What you getting at?' shot back the captive.

'I've booked you a place on the next stage, one-way ticket all the way to the Colorado border. Paid for out of council funds. You may have been wronged in the past, Spengler, but I don't want your kind in Dodge.' The terse comment brooked no rejoinder. 'I aim to make this a peaceful, law-abiding place. And that don't include kids what take the law into their own hands.'

Calloway unlocked the cell and jerked his head for Doc to leave.

'What about my gun?' asked Doc, setting his hat gingerly over the bandaged lump.

'You can have it back when I see you on that stage.' Calloway glanced at the office clock, checking the time with his own pocket-watch. 'It leaves in one hour, so you best get to packin' your things and sayin' your farewells.' His hand rested on the pearl butt of the gleaming Peacemaker. 'It wouldn't be in your best interests to miss that stage.' The thin smile held no humour.

'Much obliged for the first-class accommodation and gourmet cooking, Marshal,' retorted Doc, attempting to regain lost ground as he stepped out on to Front Street.

'All part of the service.'

The crisp reply followed him down the street.

SEVEN

NEW BEGINNINGS

The evening stage was being loaded. Doc was the only passenger. So far. Idly he surveyed the busy thoroughfare of Front Street. It didn't smell so bad once you had gotten used to it, even though the piles of buffalo hides never seemed to get any smaller. Nor did the constant bellowing of recalcitrant steers being herded along the side of the tracks down to the loading depot.

He puffed on his last cigar – a parting gesture from Buckskin Bob, along with his pistol. Then he noticed the hulking figure of Clipper Jim Tandy swaying along the far boardwalk. He was warbling a sea-shanty, and affecting the rolling gait adopted by all matelots to assist their safe passage along the heaving decks of their ships. The strange sight brought a grin to Doc's drawn features. He needed to have something to smile at after the dire mishap of almost blowing out an innocent man.

The guy was heading down to the Long Branch. Doc tipped his hat as they locked eyes across the street. Tandy scowled, ignoring the offered pleasantry. Forgive and forget was not in his vocabulary where Doc Spengler was concerned.

Doc shrugged. Maybe in Colorado he would have more luck. He surely was in need of that lady's helping hand. As he pondered on the coming journey his ruminations were interrupted by stridently raised voices of the female variety.

He peered out from the window of the stagecoach. Trundling down the street were a dozen agitated matrons from the more respectable side of the tracks. And judging by the vociferous output, they were none too pleased.

Curiosity softened Doc's ashen features. The grey pallor melted to more of a russet hue.

What was causing all the fuss?

Then he saw her.

Ginger LaPlage. In the middle of the bustling retinue.

Doc released a hearty chuckle. Out loud this time. In all the hurly burly, he was unable to comprehend what was being said. Though clearly, the good ladies of Dodge City were none too pleased with some as yet mysterious aspect of the singer's conduct. Another raucous bout of laughter burst from Doc's gaping maw. It seemed that he and Ginger were destined to be thrown together, literally.

The procession was met outside the Overland depot by the mayor and other members of the town council.

Ginger was hustled to the front of the gathering, her clothing in total disarray, a ridiculous pillbox hat perched askew on her rampant mass of red curls.

'Let go of me, you bunch of flat-chested harridans,' howled Ginger, struggling between a duo of tall beanpoles. Those behind were prodding and poking with umbrellas and broom-handles. 'How dare you treat me like this!'

Her furious exclamation received an equally robust reaction from the Ladies' Temperance League. It wasn't every day that their meetings were heckled and broken up. And by a theatrical at that. Such an occurrence was an insult to all women of a proper and genteel upbringing.

It was the mayor's wife who turned around, lifting a gloved hand to call the gathering to order. Her first remark was aimed at her husband.

'This is the . . . the person who has caused all the trouble,' spluttered Mrs Philomena Twigg, wiping mud off her face with a badly soiled handkerchief. 'Not only did she burst unannounced and uninvited into a private meeting, but she had the audacity to attack my own person in the process.'

Mrs Twigg, President of the League, was incensed. Her round fleshy face was purple with indignation, her parasol raised in threatening fashion, ready to strike down the object of her tirade.

'Now now, Philomena my dear,' soothed the mayor, attempting to extricate the flapping weapon from his wife's grasp. 'Let's all calm down and go inside to discuss the matter sensibly and without recourse to violence.'

The President huffed and blustered, insisting that Ginger be expelled from Dodge City forthwith.

'We at the Temperance League are trying to build a town fit for respectable people to live and work in,' she proclaimed stiffly, while stamping her feet, arms wafting like Independence Day bunting. 'Creatures like this have no place in our community. She and her kind bring all good-living women into disrepute.'

'That's the biggest load of pig-swill I ever did hear,' replied Ginger vehemently as they hustled her inside the depot. 'Bigoted snobs and tight fannies, the lot of you. It's no wonder your menfolk want some fun and titillation. And I can give 'em both – in generous measures as well.'

This brought a renewed outburst from the spluttering females.

Doc was enjoying every minute. This show was worth all the aggravation he had suffered over the last few days. He leaned further out of the window.

'You tell 'em, Ginger,' he yelled above the clamour. 'Give 'em hell.'

But she was already inside the depot with the mayor and Mrs Philomena Twigg. No doubt, like himself, being forcibly given a free ticket to the Colorado border. It would be just like old times.

Half an hour later the throbbing metropolis of Dodge City with all its smells and noise had faded into the background of their minds. Doc was pleased to have Ginger for company on the three-day journey. She was more fun than Buckskin Bob Calloway, Captain Tandy, or even Philomena Twigg.

Gradually she unburdened herself to him.

The Ladies' Temperance League had taken it upon themselves to tame Dodge City. They had the support of the more influential dignitaries who wanted to attract permanent business into the town. This would only be possible if the more unruly elements were neutralized. Itinerant wanderers like Doc Spengler and Ginger LaPlage were not welcome in the Dodge City of the future.

The League had duly lodged a complaint with the

mayor's office about the lewd and unseemly act being performed by Miss LaPlage at the Blue Canary Music Room. Following a visit from the town council, the proprietor had reluctantly terminated her employment.

Not one to lie down quietly, Ginger had stormed off down to the Temperance Hall where a meeting was being held. Her verbal and abusive harassment of the good ladies was met with an equally firm ejection. Not a hard task as there were twenty members of the League at the meeting.

Hustled out on to the street, Ginger had responded by throwing clods of mud at the windows. When the President emerged, she was met with a wet and juicy sample that struck her slap-bang in the kisser, if such had ever been its use.

'I bet she enjoyed that,' scoffed Doc with tears in his eyes.

'The old bird went berserk,' replied Ginger. 'She looked a right picture I can tell you. Spitting feathers she was. I nearly split my corset. And not only me. The ruckus had attracted a group of buffalo-skinners from across the tracks. That really set the cat among the pigeons.'

'They seem to have roughed you up some,' observed Doc, offering her a plug from his hip-flask.

'Nothin' I couldn't handle,' snorted Ginger, tossing her rampant locks in the air.

'I could see that,' smiled Doc. Then in a more thoughtful mood added: 'Still leaves us in a fix though.'

She gave him a quizzical look.

'We can't keep getting thrown out of every town we try to settle in.'

'Does that mean we're *partners?*'

The impishly cute grin challenged Doc to deny any such impropriety. As expected, his face reddened. Doc presented an awkward shyness that the girl found endearing, quite unlike the crude manners of the roughnecks with whom she normally associated.

'Just travellers thrown together by circumstance,' he eventually managed.

Ginger hurried on to save him further discomfiture.

'They tell me that Colorado is more tolerant towards . . .' Here she paused, flashing those big green eyes suggestively. Doc's knees trembled, his hands felt sticky. Ginger certainly had a way with her. '. . . Acts of a more revealing nature.'

'G-gambling too, I h-hope.' Doc coughed to conceal his stuttered response.

'No problems there, mister,' purred Ginger, the words flowing like melted chocolate. 'Not yet being a state, like Kansas, the place is still wide open. Just the place for the likes of you and me to make some dough.'

Her lips peeled back in a knowing smile, white teeth flashing in the sunlight. Then she laid her head on his shoulder, the long black eyelashes fluttering briefly before resting on her cheek. Doc exhaled slowly. A warm glow suffused his body. Ginger LaPlage was one helluva gal. Maybe too much for one man to handle.

This was the closest he'd come to knowing a woman since his mother had died. Sure, he'd had women, paid for their services. But really getting to know someone had thus far eluded him. For that to happen you needed to set down roots, settle in one place, get that drifter's itch out of your system. Doc had always had a hankering, a need to find out what lay over the next horizon.

*

Towards late afternoon, on the second day out from Dodge, the Overland entered a more rugged type of country. The flat grasslands of the central prairies had been left behind as the stage was forced to slow its pace on the more frequent uphill gradients.

Oceans of coarse sedge gave way to the arid scrub of yucca, gramma grass and prickly pear, interspersed with rocky outcrops. A flock of meadow-larks flew past the window. The howl of a lone coyote echoed back from the rocky ramparts that rose up on either side of the trail. Soaring pinnacles of sand-blasted orange poked at the azure firmament as the westering sun cast long shadowy fingers across the parched landscape. A lonely, brutal terrain, yet strangely calm and serene.

Not for much longer.

It happened in the blink of an eye.

A long thin shaft, flighted with the feathers of a wild turkey, buried itself in the wooden backrest not two inches from Doc's lolling head. He had been half-asleep, lulled into a lethargic stupor by the constant jog of the swaying coach. The dull thunk of the lethal barb brought him instantly awake to witness the driver flying past the window. His choking death-rattle was whipped away as the coach careered onward, now out of control.

Sticking his head out into the firing-line, Doc peered back to see a band of pursuing Indians. One had dragged his mount up short, a skinning-knife ready to scalp the spiked cadaver. Another dozen braves, yelling and hallooing, continued the chase. More arrows struck the coach, aimed at the fine target offered by Doc's stunned expression.

By this time Ginger was awake, together with the two other passengers – a rancher by the name of Dan Treacher, heading back to Santa Fe, New Mexico, after selling off his herd, and a liquor salesman, Herman Cragg, specializing in imported French wine.

Apart from Doc, who had his old Henry repeater with him in addition to the trusty Remington-Rider, only Treacher was armed.

The rancher took a fearful peep behind at the pursuing band of renegades. They were less than fifty yards back and rapidly gaining ground.

'Looks like a bunch of loose bucks have broken out of the Comanche reservation at Carson Flats,' he asserted, snapping off a couple of quick shots, none of which had any effect. 'They're painted up and after blood. That one in the front is Elk Horn. A real mean devil. I thought his bunch of rebels had been thrown in the pokey. Appears like they've gone and busted out.'

Mouthing a rabid curse, he dragged his exposed pate back inside as a well-aimed shaft skewered his new Stetson to the outer framework.

'Goldamed redskins!' The growl of indignation was more an angry retort than one of fear. He turned to face Doc. 'Someone oughta climb out and secure that team. Else them red devils is gonna feel our hair. And much more besides where the lady's concerned.'

Ginger gave an involuntary shudder.

The cowman's no-nonsense gaze fixed on to Doc's stony dial. 'I'm too old for tricks like that,' he said. 'It's up to you, young feller. What d'yuh say?'

'I will be pleased to help out if one of you gentlemen would be kind enough to lend me a firearm,' butted in the

71

drummer. The pair of Westerners ogled the speaker, mouths hung open.

Herman Cragg was small and thin with a black moustache and was dressed in a smart brown suit. He gave the impression of being a weedy greenhorn. That had been Doc's first assessment of the drummer. Now he offered the man a new look of respect. A band of Indians hollering for revenge on the white-eyes was apt to turn most men to jelly. This guy was cool as you please. He hadn't even broken sweat.

Doc handed over the Henry.

'Lever a fresh round into the breech before each shot,' he instructed, assuming the dude was a tenderfoot around guns.

'I am acquainted with the Henry 16-round rim-fire repeater,' Cragg interrupted, casually taking hold of the brass-framed rifle and expertly levering the action. 'And if I am not mistaken, this one is an 1863 model.' He looked across at Doc, eyes raised for confirmation.

'Erm, could be,' replied the gambler lamely. 'I won it off a skint miner in Abilene during a card-game.' His stunned regard was matched by that of Dan Treacher.

The latter quickly recovered his composure.

'Best get to it, son,' he said. 'Them ugly cusses is a gittin' awful close.'

Doc sighed. Ginger gripped his hand tightly, then kissed him hard on the lips.

'God be with you, Doctor Aaron Spengler.' Their eyes caressed each other. A brief yet poignant blending of hearts. Then Doc was scrambling out of the window up on to the roof of the bouncing coach.

Immediately a flurry of shots erupted from below him

on both sides of the coach. Even in the blistering heat, Doc felt a cold chill, the icy finger of dread playing with his nerve ends. He visibly shrugged off the sense of trepidation. There was work to be done. A snapped glimpse to his rear and he had the satisfaction of seeing two Indians throw up their hands to disappear over the backs of their ponies. That drummer sure knew his onions when it came to shooting.

Sliding into the bench seat, he uttered an audible sigh of relief. The leathers were still intact. He had conjured up visions of being forced to grapple amidst pounding hoofs to regain the long trailing reins. Somehow, through pure luck, or divine providence, they had become wrapped around the brake-lever.

Yipping and heehawing at the leaderless team of six, Doc took control. Even though he had never driven a stagecoach before, he figured it was no different from the Medicine Show caravan of his youth. The problem was remaining seated. Jumping and rocking like a demented roller-coaster, the coach threatened to disintegrate at any moment. It had never been designed for such extreme usage.

There was no time for worrying about that. Slapping leathers against the bucking rumps, Doc urged the team onward. He soon managed to pick up the pace and draw away from the rampant pursuers. Once he had assumed full control, the new driver palmed his own revolver, adding to the discordant barrage of shots from below.

When two more Indians bit the dust, one of them their leader, Elk Horn, the others lost their hunger for the fight. Pulling back, they watched dolefully as the Overland passed through the gap in the rocky wall known as Black

Butte Pass and so into the territory of Colorado.

A cheer went up from inside the coach.

'Yeehaw!' sang out Dan Treacher. 'That showed 'em.'

'Didn't it just!' Doc felt the muscles in his back relax as the tension eased palpably.

Hauling back to a steady canter, Doc brought the team to a halt. The four passengers descended from the coach to stretch legs and allow the heat of the encounter to dissipate. It was Herman Cragg who eventually broke the easy silence.

'My, that was some dog-fight. The only Indian I ever saw before today was in one of them Medicine Shows.' Doc's left eyebrow raised slightly, his mouth creasing at the corners into a sardonic smile. Nobody noticed.

The salesman scrambled up on to the coach roof, extricated a leather case, and handed it carefully down to Dan Treacher. Back on terra firma, he opened up the case and selected a sample of the contents.

'In view of this encounter, and our momentous victory over the noble savage,' he announced solemnly whilst uncorking a bottle of the finest red wine, 'may I invite you all to imbibe this fine vintage.' He filled four glasses and handed one to each of them. Raising his own glass, he offered them a toast. 'Your good health and long may you enjoy it.' They each returned the salute, relishing the delicate bouquet of a drink that only Ginger LaPlage had ever previously tasted. French wine was yet to make its appearance in the saloons of Western frontier society.

Doc sucked his lips, not quite sure what to make of it.

'That sure is' – he struggled to find the right word – 'different, Mr Cragg.'

'Not to your taste, sir?'

'No, no!' Doc hastened to add, slurping down the rest of the glass. 'Just that I ain't made its acquaintance before.'

Cragg sniffed, turning to Ginger. 'I see the lady knows a fine beverage when she meets one.'

Ginger purposefully offered a sophisticated twitch of her aquiline nose to the glass. An eloquent nod of appreciation was followed by a refined sip. Then, gently rolling the flavoursome draught round her mouth, she pursed her rouged lips. A gentle sigh of contentment issued forth.

Treacher and Doc Spengler stood rooted to the spot, their eyes on stalks, agog with wonder.

'Now that is one first-class tipple, gentlemen. And that's no exaggeration,' she purred, flashing her big green orbs.

Herman Cragg smirked knowingly.

'Believe me, gentlemen,' he averred, his own features warping into some hideous deformity. 'French wine is the drink of the future.' His eyes glazed over. 'Soon every drinking establishment west of the Mississippi will be proclaiming the true worth of the humble grape.'

Doc smiled. This dude would make a first-rate showman. His father would have applauded such a spirited performance.

After sampling another bottle the small entourage resumed its journey, this time at a more sedate pace. Soon the stagecoach was descending a long gradual incline into the Otero Valley where the town of Bent's Crossing was situated.

The end of the line. And a new beginning. Hopefully!

EIGHT

BENT'S CROSSING

Slick Warriner was finding it increasingly difficult to keep
a straight face. A snort of disdain rumbled up from deep
within his insides, threatening to overflow into a full-
blown hoot of derision. Not since that incredible run of
luck in Abilene had he encountered such a gullible heap
of suckers. Only in Bent's Crossing a week and already
Warriner had scooped more greenbacks than a month of
hard graft had earned him in Newton.

Catlike eyes surveyed the motley assortment of players.
There were the usual cowpokes anxious to augment their
meagre pay, the undertaker whose woebegone expression
on this occasion was for real and not merely to condole
with the mourners. And then there was the bank-manager.
The guy just didn't know when to throw in the towel.
Betting heavy pots on a pair of deuces. What a sap!

Warriner chuckled inwardly – his deadpan regard
giving nothing away. He felt almost sorry to relieve the
ranch hands of their hard-earned poke. But relieve them

he did. A guy had to earn a living somehow.

But with Banker Thorndyke it was a pleasure. You could read him like a book.

Especially now the dude was down over two grand.

Hyram Thorndyke was sweating buckets. And not due to the fetid atmosphere in the Split Pea saloon. Warriner had just answered his fifty-dollar bet by raising him another hundred. The card-sharp could see that the banker was down to his last fifty.

'Your call, Mr Thorndyke.'

The others had long since thrown in their hands. But, like all gamblers, they were mesmerized by the cards, especially when a hefty pot was at stake. Warriner held the banker with a stiff glower, his cold gaze mocking the other, challenging him to call or fold. Thorndyke mopped his brow, peered at his cards for the fifth time.

'Will you take another marker?' The request was little more than a throaty croak, thick with trepidation.

'Didn't quite catch that, Mr Thorndyke,' hissed Warriner, enjoying the banker's discomfiture. 'Remember that you now owe markers to the value of' – Warriner mentally totalled the sum – 'fifteen hundred bucks. You won't forget, will you?'

'Being the manager of the Cattlemen's Bank here in Bent's Crossing,' snapped Thorndyke, assuming an imperious tone of voice, 'I can most assuredly be trusted.'

'You'll see me then?' Warriner added, pushing another marker on to the bulging pot in the centre of the green-baize table.

The banker laid down his cards, a smug leer on his florid cheeks.

'Beat that, can you?'

Warriner's flat expression clouded, his mouth drooped at the left corner. Thorndyke smirked, reaching for the pot. But it was all a charade, a cruel jibe.

'I think you'll find that a full house beats a triple every time.' Warriner puffed on a cigar, raking his winnings into the black derby.

The oily smile rocked the stunned banker back into his seat. His fleshy jowls quivered, the red face took on a grey hue.

The gambler stood, carefully ensuring that the cards were retained in his possession. It wouldn't do for anyone to examine them too closely.

'Another time then, gentlemen,' he said brightly. 'I always give everybody the chance to win their money back. Slick Warriner is nothing if not fair.' He casually flicked a ten-dollar bill on to the table. 'You fellers have a drink on me. It might help to soften the blow.'

Just as a highly satisfied Slick Warriner was mounting the stairs at the back of the saloon, the Overland stage came to a juddering halt outside the local depot office, three blocks south of the Split Pea. A cloud of ochre dust surrounded the coach, blown every which way by a rampant wind funnelling down the street.

It was met by the agency clerk, an anxious frown clouding his features.

'Where's Whipcrack Larson?' he asked, hurrying on before anybody could answer, 'and who in tarnation are you?' This to Doc, who had expertly drawn the sweating team to a halt right outside the depot.

'The stage was attacked by a bunch of renegades,' replied Dan Treacher whilst assisting Ginger out of the coach. 'They wus Comanches and painted up like saloon Jezebels.' He quickly raised the bruised Stetson apologetically. 'No offence meant, Miss LaPlage.'

'None taken, Mr Treacher.'

'What happened to Whipcrack?'

'Skewered him with an arrow,' Doc joined in, tying off the reins to the brake-lever. 'First thing we knew about it was him flying past the open window. Then all hell let loose.'

'We were lucky this brave young man was able to climb up and control the horses.' Herman Cragg added his praise to Doc's exploit. 'Otherwise we would have most certainly come to a sticky end.'

'That was some mighty fine shooting from you as well, Mr Cragg.' Doc glanced askew at the little man. 'How come you was such a dead shot? Never seen shooting like that afore. And from a liquor salesman as well.'

'It was during the war, sir.' Cragg's tone was subdued, modest even. 'My commanding officer found out I had a quick eye and a steady hand. They trained me to be a sniper. Not a particularly glamorous task. Picking off other men from hiding. But that was the war. I'm sure we all did things that afterwards we regretted.'

Treacher offered a cognizant grunt of accord.

'I'd be much obliged if you folks could each make a brief statement for my report,' said the agent, ushering them into the office. 'Then I'll send someone out to collect poor old Whipcrack's body.' A wistful veil spread over his thin face. 'He allus claimed that none of his coaches had ever been stopped by road agents, or Indians. Took a pride in his job. Seems as how he kept his record anyway. Pity he won't be around to enjoy it no more.'

After signing their statements, the passengers went across to book rooms at the only hotel in town. Ginger made a point of ensuring that she and Doc were in adjacent rooms. After settling themselves in at the Golden Sovereign, the unlikely pair of travellers went down to the dining-room for supper.

During the meal Doc couldn't help noticing the young woman sitting at the adjacent table. Blonde hair, shimmering like a field of corn, cascaded over her slim shoulders, the curled edges bouncing with a life of their own. When visiting the ladies' room, the slender creature glided effortlessly between the tables exuding a gazelle-like elegance, a graceful rhythm of sensuous awareness.

She was attended by a much older man, well-dressed in a frock-coat and neck-tie. A diamond stick-pin testified to his affluence.

Much as the girl's physical attributes were mesmerizing to the red-blooded young man, it was her eyes that captured his attention. Bright blue, the colour of a summer sky, they ought to have been alive, flashing with youthful zest and vitality. Instead, they betrayed a forlorn, even desolate sadness. As if some bleak calamity was clutching at her heart, about to swallow this lustrous vision into its dark void.

In the whole restaurant, only Doc appeared to have sensed the girl's sorrowful distress. Outwardly calm and cheerful, there was no denying that some disturbing phenomenon was imprisoned within her soul, tearing her apart.

A psychic awareness handed down from his mother enabled Aaron Spengler to perceive underlying situations invisible to the everyday mortal. Elvira had claimed an affinity with the spirit world and used her gift to help others to communicate with the hereafter.

'What you looking at?'

The blunt question, almost an accusation, jerked Doc's thoughts back to the concrete world of satisfying the inner man.

'Eh?' Doc muttered, focusing his glazed eyes on the menu. 'Just deciding what to choose is all.'

'She ain't on the menu, if that's what you was figurin'.' Ginger slanted a dark look at the girl, even and challenging. 'Too classy for the likes of you.'

'Don't know what you mean.'

'Then screw your peepers back into their sockets, mister.'

Doc's face reddened.

The rest of the meal passed without further incident. By the time coffee was served, Doc had introduced himself as a land speculator. This revelation drew forth a painful kick from Ginger's pointed shoe beneath the table. His expression barely faltered as he established a rapport with the two diners, learning that the girl's name was Anna Thorndyke and she worked as a cashier at her father's bank.

His witty commentary appeared to distract the girl from her melancholia, albeit only temporarily. During brief lapses in the conversation, the dull ache reasserted itself in the limpid pools.

By the end of the meal, Ginger was gnashing her teeth. She was on edge, angry with herself for caring. But there was no denying the fact: she had become more than a bit fond of Doc Spengler. The green-eyed monster called jealousy was beginning to raise its ugly head.

Ginger had never let a man get this close before, and it worried her. Especially when the object of her affections was showing interest in another woman. Not any old dame either – a banker's daughter, who was extremely comely, if rather naïve as regards her attractiveness to the opposite sex.

Ginger held her caustic temper in check with supreme effort. Her smile was forced, her utterances flat and jerky. But what had she to complain about? They weren't engaged, courting, or even stepping out together. Just two travellers who had helped each other along life's bustling highway.

So it was no surprise when Doc left her outside the hotel with a casual wave, saying he was off to investigate the possibilities of setting up a game in one of the saloons.

'When will I see you again?' she called after his retreating back.

Raised arms and a careless shrug accompanied his puzzled frown. The thought crossed his mind that this gal was becoming a mite too clingy.

'See you around,' he snapped rather testily, leaving Ginger to her own devices. She was a big girl, attractive in a forward sort of way, there was no disputing, but not really his type. And anyway, she could look after herself without him forever acting as chaperone.

The church bell struck the hour. It was seven in the evening.

His first call was to the Split Pea saloon. Shouldering through the batwings, the rancid odour of burnt fat assailed his senses. And not merely from the tallow lamps strung up to the blackened roof-beams. Not the sort of place to take on victuals, he surmised. It pulled him up short. His gaze slid across to the barkeep.

Shifty eyes set too close together held Doc's steady appraisal. A bad sign. The guy's sneering assessment of this newcomer's potential raised Doc's hackles before he'd hardly set foot in the berg. He detested people who measured him in dollars, gauging how much he was worth.

'Some'n wrong, mister?' The rasping challenge issuing from the barkeep's twisted maw was like a red rag to a bull.

Doc was at the counter in two quick strides. He grabbed a drink from a nearby table and threw the contents into the skulking toad's face.

'You need a good wash, feller, along with the rest of this flea-pit,' he barked. The snivelling wretch snarled angrily, his hand straying to a hidden shotgun beneath the bar.

'Don't even think on it unless you favour a gut full of lead.'

A pregnant silence had settled over the gloomy room, the other patrons vigilant, awaiting some dramatic action. They were to be disappointed, this time. The rancid beer-puller scowled, lifting his hands above the greasy bar top.

'You're new in town, mister,' he gurgled whilst wiping his face with a filthy rag. 'Action like that's gonna git yer head blowed off.'

'Not by you, stink bomb.'

Backing out of the saloon, his right hand hovering over the gun butt on his hip, he almost collided with a passer-by.

'My apologies, sir,' he said stepping back a pace. The reactive temper was dampened just as quickly as it had erupted. 'Perhaps you could inform me if there are any half-decent saloons in this town?' The query was addressed to a suave dude in a black suit sporting a white beard in the manner of the famous hunter Buffalo Bill Cody. 'Some place where a feller ain't gonna be poisoned. And just as likely fleeced at the tables,' he added bitingly.

The older man grinned. 'I see you've made the acquaintance of Scarface Charlie,' the suit observed wryly. 'Not one of the most endearing souls in Bent's Crossing, I've had dealings with him on more than one occasion regarding fixed games.'

'Figured as much,' remarked Doc, eyeing the man uncertainly. What dealings was the guy referring to?

The tall rangy man aimed a long digit towards an establishment some hundred yards further west.

'Try the Silver Bullet. Whispering Williams runs a clean place. And he's honest. Tell him Judge Bodine sent you. Like as not it'll earn you a free drink. Then again, he might charge you double.' The legal dignitary chuckled at his own wit as he wandered on his way.

'Much obliged, Judge,' replied Doc. Now he understood. Did that mean Bent's Crossing had a resident judge? To a man of his profession, such worthies could often be less than sympathetic. Gamblers were not the most welcomed jiggers where the forces of law and order were concerned.

However, this particular legal dignitary was correct in his assessment of the Silver Bullet. It smelt positively sweet compared with the other hovel. And a cheery barman offered him a warm greeting of welcome as he entered. Even if it was on the hoarse, raspy side.

The guy had a voice that sounded like a tired bullfrog, croaky and wheezing – hence his nickname, Whispering Williams. The smile, however, that spread across his broad red face was genuine enough, revealing a set of fine even chompers.

'If the judge recommended the Bullet, least I can do is offer you a drink on the house,' said Williams, pouring them both a double measure of best 'blue label' bourbon.

Doc thanked him, resting his right foot on the brass rail while casually appraising the interior. The back mirror was well-polished and a swamper was on hand to mop up any spillages. He nodded approvingly. A well-kept house. Framed pictures of a military nature covered the walls.

Williams picked up on Doc's interest.

'Stray bullet chopped my voice-box to shreds at Gettysburg,' he croaked. 'That's me just before the battle.' He pointed wistfully to a tall, upstanding figure in dark blue proudly bearing the epaulettes of a cavalry captain. A far cry from the balding overweight bartender who now pulled beer for a living. Williams uttered a choking sigh, almost a sob. 'The surgeon gave me the slug as a keep-sake.' He hooked out a mangled chunk of lead on a leather strap from around his neck.

More important as far as Doc was concerned was that there was no house gambler in attendance. Only a trio of independent games were in progress.

'Any chance of taking me on as the resident card-man,' enquired Doc in a discreet tone, hurrying on when Williams's eyes narrowed suspiciously. 'I tried the Split Pea down the street, but the smell put me off. And Judge Bodine told me you run a clean house in here.'

Williams relaxed. His round features creased into a sly grin.

'That Scarface Charlie is a shyster and a crook. Ain't got no proof mind, just a hunch. Any jasper that don't wash his pumps out regular is a lowdown chiseller in my book. And I'm damn sure he waters down the beer.' Whispers sipped at the bourbon, drawing his fleshy lips over the rim of the glass appreciatively whilst lancing Doc with speculative deliberation. Finally he said; 'I run an honest house in the Silver Bullet, mister. Any cheating and I'll have you run out of town on a rail.'

The brazen challenge, hard-eyed and brittle, was met evenly by Doc.

'Fair enough,' he agreed. 'To me, card-sharps are lower than rattlers.'

Williams nodded enthusiastically. 'We split down the middle, fifty-fifty. Agreed?'

'Make it sixty-forty and you've got a deal.'

'A hustler, eh?'

'Seems only fair when it's me taking all the risks.'

'Good point,' voiced Williams, a crafty smirk creasing the leathery features. 'Sixty-forty it is then.'

'When d'you want me to start?' asked Doc, anxious to stack up some much needed funding.

'No time like the present.'

Williams pushed a new deck across the bar, followed by a box of chips.

'Here's to a successful partnership.'

Doc raised his glass.

NINE

A GRIM DISCOVERY

Located on the edge of Bent's Crossing on a low knoll, Thorndyke House was one of the few double-storey residences in town. As befitted the status of the town's bank-manager, it was a sumptuous abode, brick-built by craftsmen brought in all the way from Denver. Hyram Thorndyke had set up the bank with capital accrued from what proved to be a sound investment in the Central Pacific Railroad Company.

He had left Sacramento three years previously following the demise of his beloved second wife Agatha from typhoid fever. As he headed East his business acumen had seen the potential of Bent's Crossing as a major trading centre where two trails intersected. The one operating between Santa Fe and Missouri had been an important route for the sale and exchange of manufactured goods for over forty years. And now with the regular passage of the cattle herds trailing north from Texas up through the Pecos into Wyoming territory, the town was all set to become a prosperous junction.

All should have been well in the Thorndyke household.

And so it would have been had not the bank manager developed an irresistible penchant for the pasteboards, especially poker. It was a simple pleasure that had got out of control. An unhealthy obsession with the green baize had followed, which had now burgeoned into a full-blown addiction.

Shoulders slumped dejectedly, Hyram Thorndyke sat in his favourite armchair staring into the blazing log-fire. His hands gripped the leather arms so tightly that the purple veins bulged. He had not even bothered to light the oil-lamps. Fiery sprites danced and cavorted in the great stone hearth, their flickering contortions reflected in the distraught banker's lifeless, glassy eyes.

What was he to do? Warriner had threatened to inform the mayor of his indiscretions if the loss-markers were not honoured. He had been given forty-eight hours to pay up, or else! The consequences were unthinkable. All his savings had been spent on the house. There was no way he could find three grand in time.

Unless!

There was always the money in the bank safe. He had borrowed cash before to pay off debts. But nothing as big as this. If he didn't do something, and fast, his name would be mud, his daughter shunned, and it would prob-ably mean a lengthy term in the state pen. And at his age, he doubted that he would be able to handle the harsh regime.

His brow furrowed as he wrestled with his conscience.

So long as nobody wanted a hefty withdrawal in the next couple of weeks, he could borrow sufficient funds from head office in Denver to repay some of it. A bit of extra pressure on debtors to repay loans. Maybe some foreclosing, and he would be in the clear. He had no choice.

Thin lips drew back into a lurid smile. That was the answer.

Anna had been watching her father for five minutes. During that time he had not moved a muscle. Just sitting there in the dark. Something was definitely wrong. He had been acting strangely for weeks. Snapping at the least thing, testy and cantankerous. Certainly not the kind, caring father she was used to.

It all stemmed from his meeting with that odious gambler. Ever since that slimy dog had arrived in town and invited him to play a 'friendly' game of cards in the Split Pea, her father had slowly yet inexorably begun to change.

'What's wrong, Dad?' she asked, a sad inflection in her voice.

He remained silent. Only a slight lift of the shoulders indicated that he had heard.

'If you don't tell me, how can I help you?' she continued, approaching his chair.

Hyram Thorndyke turned to face her. His face was strained; waxy, dark circles beneath the flat eyes made him look ten years older.

'It's nothing, my dear. I haven't been feeling too well lately, that's all.'

'Then go to the doctor. He will give you something.'

'Just a touch of the ague. It will pass.'

His attempt at reassurance was met with a sceptical response. Her tone hardened.

'I don't believe you. You're in trouble. What is it?'

Startling her, Thorndyke leapt to his feet.

'Mind your own business. This has nothing to do with you.' His harsh rasp found her staggering back, shocked. Tears welled in the deep pools of her eyes. This wasn't the father she knew and loved. It was a stranger. 'Just leave me alone,' he barked, striding purposefully over to the door. 'I'm going out and won't be back for dinner.'

'You're going to the Split Pea. Aren't you? Gambling again.'

Her accusation, low and even, bit hard. Hyram shot her a brutal, even hateful glare, sputtering inarticulately.

'If you must know, I'm going to the bank,' he rapped tersely. 'There's some unfinished business that needs attending to before the morning.'

Then he was gone, the slammed door rattling the window-panes.

But Anna was not about to give up. She determined to follow him.

Allowing her father five minutes, she then set off in pursuit. The bank was in the centre of Bent's Crossing at the intersection of Lamar and Animas Streets. There was no light showing at the front. Anna peered around, then quietly slipped down a side passage. A cat screeched, disturbed in its noctural foray in search of supper. Anna dispelled her own outburst and pounding heart. The bank's rear door was locked. But as an employee she had her own key. It turned silently in the lock. Cautiously she opened it adjusting her gaze to the darkness of the back room.

Ahead of her, a thin sliver of yellow light beamed from beneath the door leading into the main office. In the distance, everyday sounds of a town going about its normal business lent an eerie dreamlike quality to the bizarre situation. A tightness in the throat, a trembling of loose muscles pinned Anna to the spot. What would she find beyond that door? Were her fears all wrong? Was her father merely off-colour, and this visit to the bank a mundane piece of business? These and a hundred other questions flashed through her frazzled brain.

There was only one way to find out.

Taut nerves were stretched to breaking-point as she slowly turned the handle and gently pushed the heavy oak door. Oiled hinges ensured a silent opening. And there he was, hunched over the smaller of two iron safes.

Anna suddenly realized that she had been holding her breath. She drew in a deep lungful of air, then deliberately exhaled loudly. Instantly the man rifling the safe jerked his head round, dropping the bundles of notes he had been about to secrete in a black leather bag.

'What are you doing here?' he demanded, the hoarse crackle in his voice betraying the shock at being discovered robbing his own safe.

'It's me that should be asking the questions, Father,' Anna blurted, stunned that her own kin was a . . . a thief. 'What are you doing with that money?'

For a brief instant Hyram Thorndyke was lost for words. But he quickly recovered his composure. Having proved himself adept at slithering up the greasy pole of the financial world by means of a smoothly devious tongue, he felt well able to handle a suspicious daughter.

'This is a private matter, Anna,' he asserted firmly, 'and no concern of yours.'

'It is my concern if you sneak out of the house at night—'

'I was not sneaking,' he interrupted.

'—to take money from the safe.' Anna ignored the retort. She paused, then repeated her question, this time in a low accusing tone. 'Why are you taking that money from the safe. As the cashier, I should be informed of all such transactions.'

Thorndyke was thrown by his daughter's self-confident, pushy manner. He was also irritated by it.

'That is no business of yours. I am the manager and not answerable to anyone else for my actions.' His voice was sharp and edgy with menace. 'Now go home and stay out of things that do not involve you.'

She held his look, evenly and firm.

'It's for that gambler, isn't it?'

'I don't know what you're talking about' The reply was too quick, too snappy.

'Yes you do,' she shouted. 'You've been playing cards again, haven't you?' A note of anxiety had crept into her accusation, an acute worry that her father was drifting into deep water without a paddle. 'How much have you lost this time?' Her voice had cracked with the strain. It was almost a sob, a cry for help.

Thorndyke leapt to his feet, threw down the bag and grabbed Anna's arm. A determined hardness shone in his eyes, matched by an ugly snarl.

'I told you to keep your nose out.'

A sharp crack followed.

Anna was taken completely by surprise. She screamed, clapping a hand to her burning cheek. It was the first time her father had ever laid hands on her in such a violent manner. She cringed, stumbling back away from this awful monster.

The instant his hand had lifted to strike, Hyram had regretted the action. It was as if some evil demon had taken control of his mind, forcing his hand. His shoulders slumped, the cold look dissolved as fear and remorse took hold.

'I'm sorry, Anna.' The words choked in his parched throat. 'I didn't mean to . . .'

But it was too late. His daughter had dashed from the room.

That night Anna locked herself in her room, refusing all entreaties by her father to come out and discuss the matter. Hyram had wheedled, begged and pleaded with her to forgive him. All to no avail.

Next day she did not go to work. Her mind was in a turmoil of unresolved emotions: one minute angry and frustrated, the next worried and fretful. One thing was for sure. It was no use staying locked away hoping this horrendous nightmare would resolve itself.

The Lord helps those who help themselves.

It was an adage preached by the Reverend Fosbury only last Sunday.

Once determined on a course of action, Anna Thorndyke displayed an indomitable spirit that could be described as stubborn and hard-headed. It was an admirable, if sometimes ill-considered, quality that her father had come to accept rather reluctantly. Slipping on a topcoat and bonnet, she issued from the family home, determined to prevent him from tumbling into the abyss.

Help was needed. Thorndyke had two close friends. Throwing, herself on the mercy of Judge Bodine was out of the question. There was no way she was going to confide in the law until all other options had failed. Then there was Whispering Jake Williams. This unlikely friendship had been formed while they were shipmates on the infamous Cape Horn run between New York and San Francisco following the '49 gold-rush. That had been in her father's youth, before he had settled down, worked hard at improving himself and eventually become respectable.

Hyram had met his second wife in Sacramento when Anna was only six years old. She had often asked him why they had left Missouri so suddenly following the death of her mother. But he had remained tight-lipped refusing to throw any illumination on to this aspect of his hazy past. All she knew for certain was that he had been a sailor, and as such, away from home for months at a time.

Ten minutes later she cautiously pushed open the swing-doors of the Silver Bullet, casting a wary eye over the interior. At that time of day there were few customers to be seen. A trio of cowhands were lounging at the bar, a red-headed singer was practising with a small group of musicians at the back, a couple of fellows were shovelling food into their mouths as if there was no tomorrow, and a lone guy was shuffling cards at a table.

She eyed the dexterity of the card wielder, openly scowling. Another gambler. The man had said he was a land speculator when he had introduced himself over dinner the other evening at the Golden Sovereign. He had seemed such a presentable fellow.

Jake Williams was cleaning glasses at the bar.

'Mornin' there, Miss Anna,' he called on noticing her hovering by the doors. 'What brings you here at this time of day? Figured you'd be at the bank.'

The singer curtailed her warbling and arrowed the

newcomer with a baleful stare.

Doc forgot about the game of patience. His interest was aroused. Yes indeed. What could the banker's daughter be wanting with the saloon-owner in the middle of the day? The girl's eyes were red, her satin features pale and tired, as if she'd been crying. She seemed even more anxious than the last time he had seen her, in the hotel restaurant. Something was amiss.

Edging over to the end of the bar she beckoned Williams to join her. Doc couldn't hear what was being said, but the bartender's ribbed frown informed him that glad tidings were not being dispensed. He ushered the girl over to one of the private booths located to one side of the bar.

Doc cast a languid gaze towards the other customers. Nobody had taken any notice of the girl. Only Ginger appeared less than impressed by the girl's sudden appearance. He gestured for her to continue with the practice, then sidled over to the adjacent booth. Only a heavy brocaded curtain separated them, not sufficient to prevent him from hearing most of what was being said.

'It's Dad,' began the girl. Then she seemed to freeze.

'Go on, miss,' said the barman in his hoarse, whispering lilt. 'I'm all ears.'

Then it all emerged, a tumbled outpouring of mixed emotions – grief, sadness, anxiety, resentment.

'Why did he have to get mixed up with gambling, especially in a dive like the Split Pea. Its been going on for weeks. I thought he was only playing for low stakes, loose change. Clearly I was wrong.'

'How deep is he in?' enquired Williams.

Anna drew in a sharp breath.

'He says no more than one thousand dollars,' she groaned, wringing her hands, 'but I know it's more, much more. He was jamming huge wads of notes into that hold-all when I caught him. There must have been about three thousand in all.'

A low whistle issued from the barman's fractured larynx. It sounded like a coyote in mourning.

'If he owes Slick Warriner that much *dinero*, he really is in bad trouble. I'd loan him the money if I had that much but . . .'

Doc's mind was spinning. So that was it. The banker had a mountain of unresolved markers that needed redeeming. The rest of the heart-rending spate was lost on the young gambler.

Slick Warriner! Here in Bent's Crossing.

Soon after, Anna Thorndyke left with the hesitant assurance that Jake Williams would have words with his friend and try to resolve the unsavoury matter without recourse to the law, if that were possible.

Later that night, after the bar had closed, Doc decided to confide the grim news to Ginger. Naturally she was suspicious, and less than sympathetic, until he told her that Slick Warriner was at the bottom of it all.

'I'm danged certain he's been fleecing that jackass of a banker,' he said, 'And now the dude's robbing his own bank to pay Warriner off.'

Ginger shook her head, the rampant tresses shimmering fierily in the dim lamplight. 'Serves him right. That's what I be saying,' she pouted, stiffly aloof.

'But what about Anna?' responded Doc cautiously. 'She don't deserve to be labelled as the daughter of a thief.'

'Oh!' spouted Ginger petulantly, 'Anna is it, now!'

96

'Well if you won't back me up for her sake, then do it for me. Remember it was Warriner who robbed me and had me beaten up back in Newton.' He gave her his most hangdog look, lips quivering like a jelly-fish. Narrowed eyes peered at her, anxiously willing this feisty Irish colleen to succumb to his cajoling.

'OK, I agree,' she eventually concurred. 'But only for you.'

Doc grabbed her shoulders, kissing her hard on the lips. She eagerly responded.

'I'll go see the marshal first thing in the morning and get him to arrest Warriner on a charge of robbery with violence.' Then he was gone, disappearing up the stairs to his room.

Ginger sighed. What did that skinny gal have that she didn't?

TEN

INTO THE SNAKE PIT

A sharp rap on the reinforced oaken door elicited a brisk reply.

'Door's open, and coffee's on the boil.'

Doc stepped inside the sheriff's office. It was tidy and clean, unlike many others he had been privy to. No spittoon in the corner overflowing with hawked effluent. Papers were stacked neatly in trays marked 'in' and 'out', another displayed a question-mark. The plank floor was at that moment being vigorously swept by an old dude sporting a grizzled salt-and-pepper moustache, his battered blue hat a relic from the War.

And most important of all, no idle lawdog with his rowelled boots chewing at the wooden desk. Frank Delmar was efficiency personified. A place for everything and everything in its place, from the stack of well-oiled rifles to the dapper lawman's black attire – frock-coat, creased trousers and neck-tie. He was a stocky clean-shaven individual, well-rounded and clearly a man who enjoyed the good things that life had to offer.

A noisy quill-pen scratched across a document.

'Help yourself to coffee.' Delmar uttered the abrupt invitation without looking up from his work. 'Be with you in a minute.'

Doc nodded approvingly, obeying the bidding. He was even more certain that help would be forthcoming after tasting the potent brew. Strong and thick, but not stewed, just as he liked it.

Five minutes later the sheriff interrupted Doc's avid interest in the display of Wanted posters.

'What can I do for you then, Mr Spengler?'

Doc spun round.

'You know me?' His tone was one of surprise.

'Always make it my business to git the lowdown about strangers in town,' said Delmar, helping himself to a mug of coffee. 'You're shacked up with a singer called Ginger LaPlage.'

'You should tell your informant to get his facts right'

'Yeah?'

'Miss LaPlage and myself are just good friends, more like travelling-companions,' crowed Doc, a hint of amusement crinkling his face. 'And that's all.'

Delmar uttered a curt grunt.

'So what is it you want?' he rapped, gruffly impatient and to the point.

'There's a gambler over at the Split Pea name of Slick Warriner.'

Delmar waited, his keen gaze carefully appraising the visitor.

Doc returned his stare evenly, then continued: 'He's big trouble. Had me done over, then robbed me of my winnings. It was only through the timely intervention of Miss LaPlage that I escaped with my life.' Tight-lipped, Doc narrowed his eyes. 'I want you to arrest him and clap him in the hoosegow.'

Delmar stroked his chin, considering Doc from beneath heavy black eyebrows.

Then he said: 'Bin no reports of any such robbery in this town. Nor even the county.'

'That's 'cos it was in Newton.'

'Newton, Kansas?'

'Yep.'

Delmar shook his head. 'Cain't help you.' The statement was blunt, emphatic. The sheriff dropped his gaze back to the papers on his desk.

Doc looked him over, disbelief registering on his face.

'Why not?'

Delmar shrugged impatiently. 'Out of state. This is Colorado. I have no jurisdiction over any offences committed in other states.' For him the matter was now closed.

It took another ten minutes for Doc to reach the irreversible conclusion that no amount of persuasion or threats to seek redress from a higher authority were going to change the sheriff's mind. The law was the law. And that was that.

Dejectedly, he made to leave. Then a thought strayed into his mind.

'One thing that ain't outside your sway, Mr Delmar.'

The sheriff looked up without speaking.

'I'd be obliged if during the many and varied legal activities you *are* allowed to perform,' a strong element of sarcastic inflection lent an acerbic bite to his tone, 'you would kindly keep a look-out for a one-eyed, left-handed seaman with a Jolly Roger tattooed on his left forearm.'

Delmar sighed. He was becoming more than a touch irritated by his visitor's persistent attitude.

'And why is this dude so important to you?'

Doc's eyes became mere slits, black as pitch and icy-cold. He leaned forward, slamming a balled fist on the tidy desk. The sheriff's coffee leapt in the air, spilling across various papers. 'That, Mister Sheriff, is the man who killed my father. He may have been gunned down in Missouri, but I aim to see his killer pushing up the daisies whatever the goddamned state. And I intend it to be done legal-like.'

Delmar was none too pleased. His rounded features twisted into a hard grimace, colouring to a bright puce. In a trice he was on his feet, reaching across the desk to grab Doc's jacket.

The two men glared at each other.

'I don't give a donkey's dick who topped your pa,' snarled the lawman in a low voice oozing menace. The hot fetid breath on Doc's face turned his stomach. 'Colorado law says it ain't our affair and that's that.' Regaining a measure of control, the sheriff released his grip on Doc's collar and began dabbing a cloth at the rapidly staining papers. 'Now you best get out of here pronto, mister, afore I lose my temper and throw you in the pokey for wastin' my time.'

Doc gave a terse laugh, but remained tight-lipped. He had said his piece, and now realized there was no help forthcoming from this direction. Swivelling abruptly on his heel, he left the jailhouse, deliberately slamming the door. He was fuming, mad as hell, and needed a strong drink – maybe a few – to calm his distraught nerves.

His legs felt like jelly. Passing the open door of the Split Pea, he cautiously surveyed the interior. Warriner was over in the corner running a game. Doc's whole body stiffened, muscles tight as a drum. His head felt like a barrel of gunpowder ready to explode. He was all for stampeding in there and calling the bastard's hand, grabbing his dues and hightailing it for pastures new.

But that sort of action wasn't going to be any help to Anna Thorndyke and her father. He'd be on the run with that rat-arsed sheriff on his case, and no nearer running his father's killer to earth. With these thoughts whirling round inside his head, he pulled back from the brink. Shaking the demons free, he stumbled off back to the Silver Bullet, and a measure of sanity. At least Ginger would offer him a sympathetic ear. And probably more if he were to ask.

That night, Doc hardly slept a wink. The nightmarish scenario of Doctor Jeremiah's death returned with a vengeance. More than once he yelled out, struggling to wakefulness and bathed in sweat. The darkness brought all his demons out into the open. Especially now that he was in such a quandary regarding Anna Thorndyke. This girl had really got under his skin. He was totally smitten. Even though the two had barely exchanged more than half a dozen sentences, she had cast her spell over the young man.

But what chance had he with such a radiant creature? He was himself a gambler, just like her father. She would cross to the other side of the street to avoid such an odious breed. His only hope was to prove his intentions were honourable. He splashed water over his burning face and began pacing the room above the saloon.

As the first slivers of light heralded the dawning of a new day, he had thought of a plan of action that might work. But the effort had completely frazzled his brain. Bone-weary, he lay down and slept like a dog until well into the afternoon.

'You must be crazy!'

Ginger stamped her feet in frustration after listening to Doc's scheme to recover Hyram Thorndyke's lost money. 'And you think you can just walk in there and snatch the dough? Slick Warriner is a crafty conniving weasel. You'll only be getting yourself killed,' she ranted, waving her arms frantically. 'And for what? So some stupid knuckle-head who should know better can have his bacon saved.'

Doc answered calmly and with a firm resolve. 'Anna is at her wits' end, real upset that her father will be branded a thief,' he said. 'If I don't help her out, he'll be arrested and is bound to be sent to jail.'

'You're only doing this because of the girl,' sneered Ginger. 'She's got you caught, hook, line and sinker. Admit it!'

Doc huffed some, then had to agree.

Picking up her voluminous skirts, Ginger stormed to the door. Her head was held high, a look of disdain cracking the garishly decorated visage. But inside, her heart was bruised and bleeding.

'Do what you have to do,' she sobbed. 'See if I care.'

But she most certainly did.

It had to be that night, while Warriner was working the

tables in the Split Pea.

As he straightened his hat Doc's gritty contours were fixed in a hard mask of determination. Cautiously he made his way along Animas into the residential quarter at the north end of town where his quarry had rented a house. Eagle-eyes flicked to right and left, piercing the gloomy shadows in search of any suspicious movements. An owl hooted, setting his teeth on edge.

On reaching his objective he was pleased to note that the place was in darkness. Nevertheless, he waited five minutes to ensure that nobody was around to disturb the task he had set himself. Then, like a wraith, he slipped round to the rear, searching for some easy means of entry. All the doors were locked, the sash windows closed.

There was only one answer.

Using his elbow, Doc jabbed stiffly at one of the glass panes. It shattered inwards with a loud crash, the tiny slivers clattering on the bare floor boards. Doc held his breath, face muscles tight, fists clenched.

Nobody appeared to have heard. Reaching through, he slid the catch back, raised the sash and clambered through into the parlour. Now where was that card-sharp likely to stash his ill-gotten gains? Like as not upstairs in his bedroom. Not daring to light a match, he felt his way through into a hallway and along to the staircase. With pantherlike tread, he mounted the stairs to a veranda above. His eyes now adjusted to the opaque gloom, he could just discern that there were three rooms.

The first was a cluttered storeroom full of junk. The second a small bedroom with only a tiny dresser and chair. It was the third that offered most potential. This was clearly Warriner's private room. And it was locked!

104

Doc uttered a stifled curse. He would need to force it open. His pistol would have done the job immediately, but the loud report might attract unwanted attention. He quickly retraced his steps to the storeroom. Following a brief foray among the jumble, he discovered a box of tools containing a large hammer. Just the thing.

He returned to the locked door, inserted the clawed end into the lock and twisted. A satisfying crackle of splitting timber brought a gratified smile to his taut features. Another twist and the door burst open.

Doc prayed that the gambler had not purchased an iron safe in which to secrete his lucre. To find out he would need some form of illumination. Fumbling blindly, arms outstretched, he sidled around the large brass bedstead to a small table upon which his probing fingers located a candlestick.

Before striking a match he hauled down the window-blinds. No point announcing his presence to the whole town. Once lit, the hesitant flame flickered uncertainly, revealing a chaos of discarded bottles and unlaundered clothing. Apart from the bed there was an oak dresser, a worn leather sofa and wash-basin complete with cracked water-jug. No safe, he was thankful to see.

The dim light reflected back from a mirror in the wardrobe. Doc screwed up his nose as the musty odour bit deep. It was not a particularly appealing or homely habitat. But Slick Warriner was neither engaging nor charming. Doc nodded to himself. An ideal dump for a sneaky varmint of his ilk.

He placed the candlestick on the dresser and proceeded to rummage through the drawers and cupboards.

He found it at the back of a drawer. A metal cash-box. And weighty as well. This was what he had been searching for. He made to rise, intending to make a swift exit. And no one any the wiser as to the perpetrator of the break-in.

It was the tinkling of broken glass that attracted Magpie McGee's attention. Quickly he hoisted up his pants and left the privy at the far end of the lot. With a hefty wedge of greenbacks stashed away, Warriner had ordered his confederate to stay close to the house that night.

The gambler's intention was to quit Bent's Crossing the following day and head north for the bright lights of Denver. There was no point in hanging around now he had persuaded that knucklehead of a banker to cough up. And Judge Bodine might decide to poke his nose in and come to the conclusion that blackmail was at the bottom of Thorndyke's fall from grace. Slick Warriner had no intention of being around when the shit started flying. Awkward questions could lead to the wrong answers.

Magpie strained his ears, attempting to trace the source of the crash. He was sure it had come from the house. Was somebody trying to break in? Soundlessly, he padded back up the garden path to the house, quickly locating the broken window. He had been right. Not wishing to frighten off the intruder by stepping on the shards of glass, he hurried round to the front door and let himself in.

A brief pause to attune his senses. Above his head, muffled sounds brought a mordant curse to the thin lips of the henchman. Gritting his teeth, McGee silently mounted the staircase.

Doc Spengler was well satisfied with his night's work.

106

He would now be able to return the money that Thorndyke had handed over to the devious gambler. Anna would be so grateful. She would forget that he himself was in the same profession, enabling him to sweep her off her feet. The thought made his head whirl with excitement. They would be married and live happily ever after. A proper home for the first time in his life.

Now maybe, the fairy tale would become reality.

It came as a brutal shock to Doc's system when a harsh, discordant voice ripped through his fanciful musings.

'Just put that box down on the table,' rasped Magpie emphasizing his command with the added incentive of a cocked .36 New Model Army Colt. 'Then move into the centre of the room so's I kin get a good look at you.'

Doc froze, too stunned to move.

'I said shift yer ass, tinhorn,' snarled the little weasel, edging forward. 'Else I'll plug yer mangy hide fulla lead.'

In slow motion, Doc made to place the cash-box down, his black eyes wide and staring. He shuffled into the light cast by the dancing candle-flame.

'You!' exclaimed Magpie, appraising the intruder with a stunned look. 'We figured to send you off on a wild-goose chase to Wichita. How d'yuh track us down?'

'Luck of the devil.'

'Well, it's Old Nick you'll be callin' on perty damn quick,' snarled the hard-boiled runt. 'Now hook out the six-shooter and drop it into that water-jug. And make it slow an' easy.'

Doc had no choice but to comply. The gun dropped with a splash into the jug. As quickly as his dream had been shattered, his mind was figuring a way out of this predicament. But the Magpie's beady orbs followed his every move. He needed a distraction to turn the tables on the sneaky varmint.

Keep the guy talking. Throw him off guard.

'You and Warriner still up to your old tricks then?' enquired Doc, affecting a blasé quality in his voice. Without waiting for a reply, he quickly continued: 'What was it this time? Marked cards, or the spyglass routine?'

'What yuh talkin' about?'

'Thorndyke and his markers.' Doc was carefully watching the weasel, waiting for an opportunity to jump him. 'Nobody could have lost three grand in an honest game, and in such a short period of time. You must have been working a scam.'

'That ain't no concern of yours,' jabbed McGee. 'What's more to the point is that the sheriff will be mighty interested in me catchin' a robber. And red-handed too. Seems like you're gonna be on bread an' water for one helluva spell.' Magpie laughed harshly.

Doc's gaze hardened. He quickly picked up on the slight lowering of the Colt's long barrel. A sure sign of over-confidence. This was his chance. Maybe the only one he would get. He tensed himself and flung the cash-box at Magpie. The sharp steel edge caught the runt's gun hand, eliciting a startled yelp.

The weapon spun out of his grasp, skittering across the floor into a shadowy recess beneath the bed. But the pesky little critter was no pushover. Before Doc had a chance to recover, Magpie had whipped a lethal Bowie knife from a sheath attached to his right boot.

Snarling like a maddened polecat, he leapt across the intervening gap, stabbing at Doc with an overarm lunge. The steel blade glinted in the flickering light, missing him by a cat's whisker. Doc grabbed the knife arm as the two combatants crashed to the floor. Over and over they rolled, the wiry Magpie squirming like an eel in an attempt to loosen his opponent's grip. Doc hung on steadfastly. He knew that the little guy would rip his guts out if he got the chance.

But McGee had not worked the frontier saloons of Kansas without learning a thing or two. He allowed his lean frame to go slack allowing Doc to drag him upright and letting the other man think he had him at his mercy. Once both combatants were on their feet Magpie let fly a couple of straight jabs that connected with Doc's jaw while jamming his knee upwards towards Doc's vitals.

It was the gloomy light that saved Doc from serious and maybe terminal injury. Slightly wrong-footed, the deadly kneecap glanced off Doc's thigh. It sent a numbing jolt of agony coursing down his leg. He shook his head to clear the woolliness and cursed volubly. Desperately, knowing that his very life depended on it, he pushed the weasel away. Then, staggering back, he fell across the bed as the little rat sprang forward, the deadly blade raised for the killing strike. Magpie whooped and hollered, flecks of spittle bubbling from his open maw.

'This is where you meet yer maker, dog's breath,' he howled. A maniacal leer creased the hatchet face.

But once again Doc somehow managed to evade the plunging Bowie. He felt the rush of air as it whistled past his ear. Rolling across to the far side of the bed, he fell to the floor, his right leg still deadened from the stunning blow. Unable to stand, he lay there splayed out as McGee screamed at him like a rabid hound from hell. A lopsided glower split the gaunt face.

Doc was at his mercy.

Was this to be his final curtain call?

Not yet awhile.

Doc's hand fastened on to the runt's discarded shooter at the same moment that McGee dived across the bed, his apelike arm reaching with the eight-inch blade. Doc swung the Colt fanning the hammer. Flame and lead erupted from the revolver in a single lethal blast until it clicked on empty, the entire cylinder slamming into the lunging torso. Blood fountained from five punctures as McGee fell dead, the shattered corpse twitching a few times before it lay still.

The acrid stench of burnt cordite filled the room.

Guttural rasps stuck in Doc's dry throat as he sucked in fresh oxygen. Every muscle in his body was trembling. It wasn't every day that a man came this close to signing off.

ELEVEN

MIXED FORTUNES

Doc left the house the way he had entered. No sense tempting fate. Nobody appeared to have been alerted by the gunfire. But that was not to say that curious eyes were not at that moment peeping from behind drawn blinds in the vicinity. The moon chose that minute to slide from behind a blanket of cloud, bathing the neighbourhood in an ethereal glow.

Consequently, he took a meandering route back into the centre of Bent's Crossing. The all-important cash-box was tucked under his coat, his wide-brimmed hat pulled well down. He entered the Silver Bullet by the rear entrance, slipped up the stairs and into his room. Ginger was waiting. Her tense features registered alarm.

'Where have you been?' she spluttered. 'I've been worried sick.'

Dark circles around Doc's eyes confirmed the acute strain of the recent traumatic events.

'Gimme a drink,' he shot back, ignoring her disquiet

and slumping on to the bed. He grabbed the proffered bottle and imbibed a stiff measure. 'That's better,' he sighed as the tension eased from his tight muscles.

'Well?' persisted Ginger, snatching the bottle away.

Slowly the truth emerged, assisted by frequent belts from the whiskey-bottle. The only fact he chose to omit was the killing of Magpie McGee. The fewer people who knew about that the better.

'Anybody see you?' enquired Ginger.

Doc shook his head. His eyes flickered blankly, dulled by the liquor. Then he lay down on the bed and was sound asleep before his head hit the pillow. He was still clutching the cash-box in a vicelike grip. Gently, the singer covered him with a quilt.

'Will you ever learn?' she murmured to herself. 'This guy has eyes only for that snooty Thorndyke gal. He ain't interested in you. Not in that way at least.' Her large green eyes misted over, a single teardrop tracing a pattern down her cheek. Roughly she brushed it away, then bent down and kissed him tenderly on the forehead. 'Sleep well, my lovely paladin.'

Head bowed, shoulders drooping, she left and returned to her own room.

It would be an understatement to say that Slick Warriner was shocked when he finally returned home in the early hours of the morning. Not so much on account of his sidekick's getting himself shot and killed – there were always plenty more where Magpie had come from – but more from the fact that his cash-box had been stolen.

Warriner's face adopted an ugly scowl. A frigid scream of rage echoed round the bedroom. And he knew exactly who was responsible. That bloated heap of dung – Hyram

G. Thorndyke. Well, Mister goddamned Thorndyke, you ain't gonna get away with pullin' the plug on Slick Warriner. No sirree!

The gambler was in the parlour mumbling to himself. Pacing up and down, he was trying to figure how the banker could hope escape legal retribution for such a crime. All the evidence would point to him as being the killer. Half the town knew he was down a heap of dough.

Or would it?

He could deny the whole thing. And who could prove otherwise? Nobody would ever believe a gambler over a respected businessman. The law would assume that the killer was in the same profession. That or an ordinary thief.

So the toady had him beaten. Warriner snapped off a virulent oath. Not if he had any say in the matter. He knew that the bank's night-safe operated on a timer and could not be opened between the hours of eight in the evening and eight in the morning. Consequently, the money would still be at the banker's house.

A plan began to form in the gambler's scheming mind. Hooded eyes narrowed to grey nuggets of lead, the jutting chin solidly intent on revenge and restitution.

Before this night was over Slick Warriner would be shot of this town and well on his way north. The fleshpots of Denver beckoned invitingly. And with plenty of dough in his pockets, he envisaged no problem enjoying himself.

The thought elicited a harsh chortle from the wily gambler.

Then he quickly sobered. What about the girl? Anna Thorndyke could easily stymie his plans. She was a head-strong female and unlikely to sit idly by while some interloper robbed her father. He had to get her out of the way.

Warriner's brow ribbed in thought. She would need to be called away on some pretext. Then a flash of inspiration lit up his pallid features.

It was four in the morning when Anna Thorndyke was woken by a thudding on the front door. Her father had been drinking heavily all night. Stress and anxiety regarding his predicament had taken its toll. He was a shadow of his former self and had finally passed out around midnight. There was no chance of his surfacing before the following afternoon.

Again the urgent knock from below.

Anna wrapped a housecoat around her slender frame, lit a candle and hurried downstairs. On opening the door, she was confronted by a small boy clutching a note in his grubby paw.

'A message for Miss Thorndyke,' he said, handing her the slip of paper.

Anna read the pencil scrawl, her eyes widening as the import of the contents became clear.

'Any reply?' asked the urchin, holding out his hand.

Anna shook her head, a glazed expression bathing her anxious features. Once again she read the message.

Dear Miss Thorndyke, Prince has suffered a major heart failure and has collapsed in his stall. Please come immediately to Cody's Livery Stable as an operation is essential if he is to survive. Yours, Isaac Pennyman – Veterinary Practitioner.

During his numerous poker engagements with Hyram

Thorndyke at the Split Pea, Warriner had discovered that the banker's daughter was an avid horsewoman and her prize possession was an Arab stallion by the name of Prince. He had salted the information away in the back of his mind, little thinking it would be destined to play such a vital part in his future plans.

The urchin tugged at Anna's coat as she stood there dumbfounded. Their eyes met, the kid wagging his hand. Anna nodded absently, then shut the door, oblivious of his hint that a tip should be forthcoming. Angrily, the boy kicked the door, then turned and shuffled off into the darkness.

Hiding round the corner, Slick Warriner chuckled. The kid had already been well-paid. Now all he had to do was wait for the girl to leave on her groundless errand of mercy. Five minutes later he had the satisfaction of seeing her hurrying off down the hill towards the town.

The livery barn was at the far end. Time enough for him to locate the *dinero* and hightail it before she discovered that the message was a hoax. And if she didn't find anything amiss until the morning, he could be well out of the county and on his way north by then.

Warriner scurried over to the front door of the house. He was in luck. In her panic, she had left the door ajar. Once inside his first task was to find Thorndyke's room and get the banker to hand over the loot. This proved easier than he had expected. Voluble snoring fit to raise the devil filtered down from an upstairs room. The rhythmic grumble drew him unerringly to his objective.

Outside the study door he paused. He drew a deep breath and rushed in, brandishing a new Colt .45 Peacemaker only recently purchased. The banker was asleep in a chair.

Warriner jabbed the short barrel into Thorndyke's pudgy neck.

'Shake a leg, you son of Satan,' he hissed, standing over the recumbent form. 'Think you could get away with short-changin' me?'

Thorndyke emitted a series of grunts and snorts, but his eyes remained tight shut. Warriner grabbed him by the shirt, first shaking him violently.

'Wake up you piece of dung.'

When that produced no effect other than a loud belch the gambler snapped a vicious jab into Thorndyke's mottled face. Blood spurted from a burst nose.

Only then did the banker begin to stir.

'You drunken slob,' ranted Warriner, dragging the now groaning hulk to his feet. 'Where's the loot you stole?' A sharp back-hander propelled Thorndyke across the room. He stumbled over a chair and fell to the floor. Warriner followed up with a brutal kick to the ribs. The big man was rapidly sobering up under the harsh treatment. Another fearsome jolt in his ample midriff provoked an agonized yell of pain. 'The money, Thorndyke. Where you got it stashed? Spit the griff if'n you don't want more of the same.'

'What you talking about?' moaned Thorndyke through a split lip. He attempted to crawl away from his tormentor on all fours. 'There's only a few dollars in the safe. Here, take it.' He fished a key out of his pocket and offered it to the gambler.

Warriner quickly unlocked the iron box in the corner of the room. As he viewed the meagre contents, a bestial roar erupted from between his contorted lips. The .45 swung back towards the heavily breathing banker.

'You best own up to where you're hidin' that dough, mister,' seethed Warriner menacingly. His gaunt face was purple with rage as he added: 'Else you'll end up in the same plot as poor old Magpie.'

Thorndyke's red-rimmed eyes popped as the downstairs clock struck the half-hour. He shook his head in bewilderment. What was this skunk on about?

Warriner held the banker's petrified look.

'You've got up to the count of three, then it's bye-bye.'

The threatening barrel of the six-shooter resembled a cannon to Thorndyke.

'*One . . .*'

'I gave you all the money that was owed earlier this evening,' pleaded the banker, eyes staring mesmerized by the hovering side-arm.

'*Two . . .*'

'There is no more money. Please, you have to believe me.'

Warriner sneered as the wailing banker begged for his life. But the begging was in vain. A deathly silence followed. There was no more to be said.

Except.

'*Three.*'

'Nooooooo!'

An earth-shattering crash shook the window-frame as hot lead spewed forth. Three times the gun bucked in Warriner's clammy paw. Each time accompanied by a frenzied wail. Thick white smoke filled the room. Thorndyke clutched at his smashed chest as his life force gushed out, staining the cream carpet a rusty hue. His wide mouth flapped open like a stranded pike's, but only a stifled moan emerged. Then he slid over on to his side.

As he gasped in huge mouthfuls of air Warriner's heart was pounding in his ribcage. His gun hand shook violently. Only when the trembling finally subsided did the reality of his situation begin to register.

The leading citizen of Bent's Crossing shot dead. And nothing to show for it.

He didn't have long before the girl would return. Perhaps she would figure the message was a mistake and call on the veterinarian for confirmation. It would all take time. But not enough for him to search the whole premises.

Warriner cursed loudly as his dream of a new life dissolved before his eyes. All he could do now was return to his own house and bury that stupid varmint Magpie McGee before dawn broke. Then he would lie low and affect an air of innocence. No problem for a sharp operator used to the vagaries of poker-playing.

In the event it wasn't until late the following morning that Anna Thorndyke discovered the shattered body of her father. At first she thought the shame of his predicament had forced him into taking his own life. But the bruised and bleeding face and the lack of a weapon soon convinced her that murder of a most foul nature had been perpetrated.

She had no inkling as to the identity of the culprit. Could it be a client harbouring a grudge? An opportunist robber who figured a banker would have plenty of cash in his own home? There was no clue.

As soon as she had recovered Anna hurried off to report the killing to the sheriff.

Its situation at the meeting-point of trails meant that

Bent's Crossing was no stranger to violent confrontations. Sheriff Frank Delmar had to settle arguments regularly, sometimes with a gun. Killings were not an everyday event, and those that did occur usually involved man-to-man shoot-outs where neither party could be held accountable. Disagreements in the Western territories were often settled with a gun. It was accepted practice, and in some towns, even encouraged.

But cold-blooded murder was another ball-game entirely.

The last time Frank Delmar had dealt with such a situation was a couple of months previously when the assay office had been robbed. Clint Riley, the agent, had been gunned down when he tried to resist. It had taken him three days to die. Delmar had found no trouble forming a posse and they had caught up with the thieving skunks just before they crossed the border into New Mexico at Raton Pass.

Only one of the three killers had survived the gun battle to participate in his own necktie party. There had been a good turn-out on the day of the hanging. Delmar smiled to himself. The sheriff had been well satisfied with the outcome on that occasion. He hoped that this crime would be just as easy to solve. Elections were coming up, and another success would ensure he was re-elected for another three years.

The sheriff helped Anna Thorndyke into his buggy, then whipped up the twin black mares and headed north up the shallow rise that led to the Thorndyke residence. Delmar knew that finding the killer would be a distinct feather in his cap. Might even lead to the chance of running for mayor. He offered the girl a sideways glance.

She was trembling violently. Her distraught face showed much evidence of crying. The eyes, dull and lifeless, had withdrawn into their sockets, giving her a skeletal appearance.

The sheriff felt uncomfortable. He was glad when they reached the house. Once inside, Anna directed him upstairs to her father's study.

'Nothing has been touched,' she sobbed, her voice cracking with the strain. 'My father is just as I found him.'

'That's good, miss' Delmar nodded sagely. 'Don't wanna disturb any evidence, do we.'

'If you don't mind, I'll stay in the parlour and leave you to carry out your investigations alone,' murmured the girl, 'Mrs Bradley, the mayor's wife, has offered to stay with me until after the funeral.'

'OK by me,' agreed Delmar, mounting the stairs. 'It shouldn't take long to finish my business up there. Then the undertaker can have him.'

Once he was inside Thorndyke's study, the sheriff's nosed crinkled. The smell was overpowering. A blend of gunsmoke, a loose bowel and . . . death! He strode over to the window and threw it open, breathing long and deep. The sheriff had dealt with many a dead body during his forty-five years, but had never got used to the cloying odour that hung in the air like a dank invisible shroud.

Peering down at the shattered corpse, he frowned, a puzzled look twisting his raw-boned features. Something wasn't quite as it should be. Scratching the thick mat of greying hair atop his bullet head, he walked round the body studying it from all angles, his piercing gaze needle-sharp. Then his foot slipped on something hard and round on the floor. He bent down and picked the object up. His mouth dropped open, eyebrows raised in stunned surprise.

A glass eye!

That was it. There was a dark empty cavity where the banker's right eye should be. Instantly, his whole body tensed. Could he have solved the crime this quickly? He hardly dared to speculate. His mouth felt dry, the large platelike hands became damp and sweaty. Carefully, he rolled up the left arm of the banker's shirt-sleeve. And there it was.

The tattoo of a pirate flag!

Two out of three. All he needed was to check the last item on the list.

Slowly rising to his feet, Frank Delmar felt dazed, bemused. This was what every lawman dreamed about. But surely nothing was ever that simple. He would wake up soon and find it was, indeed, only a dream.

In the parlour he asked Anna Thorndyke the all-important question.

'Which hand did Hyram favour?' The words stuck in his throat emerging as a hoarse unintelligible prattle. He coughed to clear the obstruction. Then repeated the question. 'Was your father right- or left-handed, miss?'

Anna looked askance, puzzlement etched across her translucent face.

Delmar waited, expectantly hoping.

'He was left-handed.'

Yes!

Got the bastard! The sheriff couldn't resist a resolute cheer. Quickly resuming his stoically calm demeanour he apologized for the outburst. Then, nonchalantly he pushed his black Stetson to the back of his head, a superior

121

glint in his eye.

'Why d'you ask, Sheriff?'

'Seems like we got our man, Miss Thorndyke.'

'H-how d-did you manage that so quickly?' stammered Anna, jumping to her feet. 'How can my father being left-handed possibly assist you in identifying the killer?'

'It wasn't only that, miss,' said Delmar. 'Other information has come into my possession which means that I will be able to make an arrest within the hour.' He stood up to take his leave. 'If you would kindly come down to the jail-house in the morning I'll take your statement then and let you know who the killer is. By that time he'll be safely under lock and key in my best cell.'

On his way back into town the sheriff couldn't help pondering on how Doc Spengler had discovered the identity of his father's killer. And that particular miscreant had turned out of be one of the town's most prominent citizens, Delmar mused thoughtfully. Maybe the guy had seen the evidence for himself while visiting the bank. Or some person or persons unknown had passed on the vital details. It was of no consequence now.

So old Thorndyke had once been a seafaring man. Himself a killer too, if Spengler had been telling the truth. He had obviously managed to conceal the grisly details of his past and start a new life in Colorado.

Delmar shrugged carelessly. He had his man sure as shootin' and that was all that mattered. Now to make the arrest before the killer lit out.

TWELVE

ARREST

In effecting the arrest of a cold-blooded killer like Spengler, Frank Delmar considered it prudent to have his deputy along to back him up.

Three-fingered Charlie Branch had been a deputy for six months in Bent's Crossing. His previous appointment in Abilene, Kansas, had been literally cut short (by two fingers) in a running gun battle involving a pack of drunken cowpunchers. Rather disgruntled when their ramrod had vamoosed with the payroll, the cowhands had decided to vent their anger by shooting up the town. Charlie Branch had been caught in the middle.

Fortunately the loss of flexibility involved his left hand. But he was still grateful to Delmar for taking him on and had made no complaint when disturbed at a particularly amorous moment with Whitewash Kate upstairs in the Red Letter Pleasure Palace.

The two lawmen entered by the back door of the Silver Bullet and crept up the stairs, their footsteps silent as the grave. An oil-lamp turned down low provided sufficient illumination to inform Delmar that there were only two rooms along the corridor.

But which one contained their quarry?

Both men checked their guns. His own palmed and snapped to half-cock, Delmar indicated for Charlie to take the room on the right. Simultaneously they burst into the rooms, tense and expectant, ready for anything.

Delmar found his to be full of women's clothing and smelling like a whore's boudoir. A grumbling vision of red appeared from beneath a heap of bedding.

'What be all that row?' she spat, covering her amply exposed frontage. 'And what be you doing in my room?'

Unlike his deputy, Frank Delmar was not a man who mixed well with the opposite sex. His face coloured appreciably. Backing off he apologized, muttering something about the wrong room. Ginger wrapped a shawl round her shoulders and leapt out of the bed. She was now wide awake as the purpose of the sheriff's intrusion became apparent. If this was the wrong room, then the lawdog must be after Doc.

That was when Charlie Branch yelled out from the adjoining room.

'In here, Sheriff. I've gotten the varmint covered.'

Delmar scooted off, quickly followed by Ginger LaPlage.

'This the feller you're after?' asked the deputy, careful to maintain a beady eye on the captive.

'That's him.' The blunt retort was matched by the satisfaction plastered across his beaming face. He then addressed the man in the bed. 'Aaron Spengler, otherwise known as Doc, I am hereby arresting you on a charge of wilful murder.'

Doc's blank expression reflected total bewilderment.

'And who am I supposed to have killed?' he enquired in a flat tone.

'Doc's no killer,' interjected Ginger trying to push between the two lawmen. 'He wouldn't hurt a fly, would you, honey?'

'You keep out of this,' snapped Delmar. 'I have proof that he's nothin' but a murderin' sidewinder.' The six-shooter wagged ominously. 'And I intend to see you hang, mister.' Then he looked at the befuddled young gambler more closely. 'If he's is so darned peace-lovin', how come his ugly face is all cut up?' Grabbing Doc's day clothes that were lying on a chair, he held them up. 'And all this blood too. That ain't from shavin'.'

'Well, mister?' rapped Three-fingers, pressing forward. 'What have you to say in your defence?'

Doc was stunned, shaken, his mind all a jumbled mess. How could Warriner have known it was he who had killed Magpie McGee? He'd left no incriminating evidence behind. Nobody else had seen him entering and leaving the rented house.

Or had they?

Seeing that his captive was nonplussed, Delmar continued: 'I am arresting you for breaking into the home of the bank-manager, Hyram Thorndyke, and cold-bloodedly shooting him to death.'

Doc Spengler was now in total confusion. He was being arrested for killing the very man he had been trying to assist. He slumped back against the bedstead.

Ginger could only stare open-mouthed.

'And where is the proof of this god-awful crime?' she snapped, her square chin thrust out defiantly.

'Are you gonna tell her, or should I?' Delmar said addressing his captive. Doc remained silent, too stunned for any coherent response.

'The right eye missing and a glass bauble in its place, the left arm tattooed with a pirate's flag.' Doc's eyes widened, almost popping out of their sockets as the revelation was exposed. 'And to cap it all,' continued Delmar, 'he was left-handed. Remember what you told me over in the office? No? Well I certainly did.'

Ginger was likewise taken aback by the disclosure.

'Doc?' she croaked. 'Is this true?'

Recovering at last from the shock, his mind began to absorb the brutal truth. In a low voice, almost a whisper, he mumbled to himself: 'So Thorndyke was the killer. Thorndyke! At last, after all these years, he's paid his dues.'

Then suddenly the realization of his predicament struck home with the force of a raging tornado. He sat up, bewildered and confused. A panic-stricken look flicked between Ginger and the sheriff.

'But it weren't me,' he pleaded. 'I swear on my mother's grave. Sure I wanted him dead. But would I have told you about it, asked for your help and then gone out and done the deed straight after? I once nearly killed a feller by mistake thinking he was the one. Would have shot him down if'n I hadn't been stopped in the nick of time.' He held the sheriff's pitiless gaze. 'That was when I decided to leave it to the law.'

'Pity for him you didn't do just that. Too late now.'

Delmar gestured for Doc to get dressed.

'Take Miss LaPlage back to her room,' Delmar instructed his deputy.

When Doc was dressed, Delmar gestured with his gun for him to go ahead.

'It's the jailhouse for you. We'll be having the pleasure of your company until the next county court is in session. Judge Roscoe Bodine presiding.' Delmar's lips curled back in a mirthless smile. 'And Thorndyke was his best friend. I'm a-thinkin' he ain't gonna be too keen to find you innocent.'

The notion caused the sheriff some coarse amusement, a joke not shared by Ginger.

'Don't you fret none,' she called as Doc was clapped in handcuffs and led away. 'I'll shift Heaven and Hell to dig out the truth of this fiasco.'

A wry smirk bent Doc's mouth to one side.

Fiasco was surely the right word.

Next morning, Slick Warriner was having breakfast in the Golden Sovereign. Even though the previous night's catastrophe had left him tense and edgy, nothing was going to spoil his favourite meal of the day. He still had to work in the Split Pea but there was no way he was eating there as well. Like a red rag to a bull, the shooting of the banker had been the result of enraged frustration. Warriner had no regrets about the killing itself; just the fact that he was a hefty wedge out of pocket.

About to fork a lump of scrambled egg into his leering maw, he was interrupted by a scruffy brat. It was the same urchin who had delivered the message to Anna Thorndyke regarding the mysterious ailment to her horse. Warriner had decided that the pittance of a retainer he had to bestow on the grimy scallywag would be amply recompensed by the news he could provide. These street kids always knew everything before anyone else.

The boy tugged at his sleeve.

'You got some'n for me, kid?' hissed Warriner quietly.

'Some dude has bin arrested for bumpin' off the banker.'

Warriner's right eyebrow lifted slightly. Now fancy that, he thought.

'Has this mysterious rannie gotten a name?'

'Spengler!'

Warriner coughed, almost choking on the egg.

'Doc Spengler?'

'The very same. He's a gambler working at the Silver Bullet. Seems as how the banker had a run-in with his pa many years ago and shot him. Spengler swore to take revenge.'

So that sneaking polecat is here in Bent's Crossing. And now the jigger's in the lock-up accused of his crime. What a laugh! An evil grimace cracked Warriner's oily features.

He wiped the slivers of congealed egg from his jacket front.

'Anything else?' he snapped.

The kid shook his head.

'Well, keep yer eyes peeled.' Then as an afterthought. 'Did the sheriff recover any missing *dinero*?'

Again the kid shook his head.

A half dollar piece flipped into the air. The brat caught it one-handed, biting hard to check it was genuine. Satisfied, he pocketed the reward and disappeared through the door.

A devious thought had started to flesh itself out in the card-sharp's acute brain. Was there some connection between Spengler's sudden appearance and the missing dough? Warriner couldn't help deducing that this was the answer. Not only that: the sidewinder would be out to avenge the beating he had received in Newton. All Warriner needed to do now was figure it all out.

Easier said than done.

As soon as she had ascertained that Doc was going nowhere except the town jail, Ginger directed her steps towards Thorndyke House. She had to persuade Anna Thorndyke that the young man was not her father's killer. The evidence seemed overwhelming, but Ginger knew in her heart that Doc was innocent.

She knocked firmly on the front door. An older woman opened up and asked her business.

'I wish to speak to Miss Thorndyke urgently.'

'She doesn't want to be disturbed,' replied the woman stiffly, taking note of the garish, heavily painted appearance.

'Tell her it's about the unfortunate business with her father.'

'Any information you have should be given to the sheriff.' The woman attempted to close the door but Ginger placed her foot in the gap.

'Doc Spengler did not kill him,' pressed Ginger, trying to force her way into the house. 'Just let me speak to her. Please.' Her distraught appeal fell on deaf ears.

'No!' snapped the woman. 'Now go away.'

'It's all right, Angelina.' The thin, toneless whimper sounded like a lost soul drifting on the wind. It came from down the corridor. 'I'll speak to the lady.'

Angelina Bradley sniffed. This creature was certainly no lady. Nevertheless, she stepped aside to admit the redhead.

Once in the parlour, Ginger did her level best to win over the younger woman. Even down to admitting that Doc had become very fond of her. Would such a man then kill her father? Whatever cause he might think he had.

Anna was not convinced. It was bad enough learning that her own father had concealed a bizarre past that had included one murder, maybe even several. The thought made her break down in tears.

It was only when Ginger mentioned the recovery of her father's gambling debts that Anna began to show any signs of uncertainty.

'Doc told me all about your father being fleeced by that cheatin' skunk, Slick Warriner,' pleaded Ginger. 'And he was prepared to put his own future on the line by breakin' into the house to recover the money.'

'How did he find out? I only told Whispering Williams at the Silver Bullet.'

'Doc overheard your conversation. And decided to do somethin' about it.'

Anna's look softened. This man whom she barely knew had been prepared to place himself in danger for her family's honour.

'You mean that he has the money now?' she said.

'Sure thing. It's hid away in his room at the Silver Bullet.'

'So if Mr Spengler didn't kill my father, who did?' The girl stood up and began aimlessly pacing about the room.

'I be a-reckonin' that it had to be Warriner,' asserted Ginger firmly in her broad Irish brogue. 'Wasn't it his cash-box that had been stolen? The logical conclusion the lily-livered jigger would have reached was that your father had hired somebody to steal it back. Only a few people knew about your father's indiscretions.'

'And you were one of them.'

Anna's vehement allegation received a disdainful sniff.

'Now isn't that what close friends do? Confide in each other?' Ginger responded adding the pertinent observation: 'Anyways, Warriner probably figured that with your pa out of the picture he would be well in the clear. And with a handsome grubstake as well. What he didn't know was that Doc had lifted the dough.'

By this time Anna was willing to be persuaded.

Now only the sheriff needed convincing. And to that end, the return of the money would certainly aid Doc's cause.

Warriner had arrived at the very same conclusion.

After tossing the problem over in his devious mind, the gambler made his decision. With Spengler in the pokey, all he needed to do was get into that room above the Silver Bullet and grab the box. It had to be there.

He would need a fast horse. That black stallion of the girl's would be just dandy.

Warriner stuffed his meagre possessions into a war bag and covertly made his way over to the livery stable where the animal was kept. There he was forced to cool his heels for thirty minutes until the ostler was otherwise engaged. Then he slipped in through the open door and quietly saddled Prince. To avoid any prying eyes he led the animal through numerous back lots until he was able to tether it behind the Bullet.

Following in the footsteps taken by Delmar and his deputy in the early hours, Warriner edged carefully towards the open door. He stopped on hearing muffled noises emanating from the room. Spengler's room. And Spengler was in jail.

Somebody had beaten him to it.

Below in the saloon, laughter and the normal ribaldry associated with such establishments drifted up the stair-well. Warriner restrained the impulse to draw his pistol and rush in shooting from the hip. Instead, he slid a thin stiletto from the sheath and concealed it behind his back.

Holding his breath he peered round the edge of the door. Two women were rifling through his cash-box. The gambler's face split in a horrid rictus. And from what he could observe, all the dough was there.

'I'll take that,' he barked, stepping inside the door and quickly closing it. 'Hand it over now, else this little beauty will slice you up into dog-meat.' The blade, sharp enough to split a cat's whisker, jabbed menacingly.

Anna Thorndyke shrank back against the wall. But all Ginger could see was the repulsive specimen that was the cause of Doc's being incarcerated on a murder rap. And facing the hangman's noose.

A red pall of anger shrouded her brain, clouding any rational thinking. Savage rage, furious and chilling burst from deep within her bosom. At the same moment she lunged. Long, painted talons clawed at the grinning ogre, seeking only to tear asunder the hideous apparition before her.

Taken by surprise, Warriner stumbled back against the wall. He yelled as the sharp nails raked his pale cheeks, drawing parallel lines of crimson. But Ginger's fervid assault was cut short as the lethal dagger plunged into her stomach. A look of total surprise snatched the atavistic mask from her face. She staggered back, clutching at the

132

thin blade, buried up to the hilt. A red patch flowed rapidly across her dress.

Anna gasped aloud, but stayed rooted to the spot, paralysed with terror.

A rancorous growl spewed from between Warriner's tight lips, his cold eyes hard as ebony. He roughly pushed the dying singer aside and grabbed up the cash-box.

'She's for the angels,' he rasped, callously poking at Ginger's shivering body with his boot. Then to Anna: 'But I can't leave you here to scream blue murder.' His left eyebrow twitched in thought. 'You're comin' with me. Anybody tries to dog my trail, they know what'll happen to you.'

He drew the pistol and pretended to shoot her. Anna shrank back, a sense of awful dread writ large across her face.

'Don't worry, miss,' chuckled Warriner, holstering the gun. He knew this one wouldn't give him any trouble. And if'n she did, Jack Shiv would be put to work again. 'If all goes according to plan I'll drop you off before we hit the Pueblo rail junction. You're a good looker all right, but a heap of trouble for the likes of me. And where I'm goin', there ain't no room for excess baggage.'

His next thoughts were kept firmly within his own scheming brain. It might be better all round if he were to get rid of the girl – permanently. Just a bullet in the head while she was sleeping. The coyotes could have her for dinner. But he kept these musings to himself.

'Let's go!' said Warriner, grabbing the girl's arm. 'And not so much as a whimper if you want to see the next full moon.'

He hustled the girl along the corridor and down the

outside stairway. But the gambler had forgotten that he only had one mount. He cursed. Too late now. They would have to ride double. No problem for a stallion like Prince. But for how long? Could the horse keep up the pace indefinitely?

THIRTEEN

WHISPER WHO DARES

It was Whispering Williams who discovered Ginger. When she failed to put in an appearance at the usual evening practice with the band, he had gone upstairs to roll her out. Mumbling about inconsiderate, thoughtless women, he rapped on the door calling for her to shake a leg. Getting no response, he was about to leave when a stifled groan assailed his ears. And it was coming from Doc's room.

But it couldn't be the house gambler. The sheriff had arrested him for murdering his good friend, Hyram Thorndyke. Williams still couldn't get his head round that. But the sheriff had claimed to have a cast-iron case against the lad.

So who was in his room now?

Drawing and cocking his trusty .36 Navy Colt, Williams called out: 'Whoever's in there, come out with yer hands

high.' No response except for more groans. 'I'm comin'
in,' he warned, feeling somewhat less than confident.
'Stand back or get a gutful of lead.'

Turning the door-knob, he pushed firmly. The door
swung open. And there she was. Splayed out on the floor.
Ginger LaPlage, lying on her side in a pool of her own
blood. For a second the saloon owner was stunned, rigid
as a statue. Then his army training took over.

He removed his coat, placed it under her head and felt
for a pulse. It was there, but only just, faint and very weak.
This was no time for questions. She had lost a bucketful of
blood and needed a medical man straight away. As he
made to leave, Ginger reached for his arm. Even near to
the end her grip was vicelike.

She indicated for Williams to come close.

'Got something to tell you.' Her quavering voice was
barely more than a cracked wheeze.

'Take it easy, Ginger,' calmed Williams, matching her
straining vocals. 'Let me get you a doctor.'

'No time fer that,' she insisted. Flickering embers still
smouldered in her vacant eyes. 'Warriner did this . . . stole
back Thorndyke's money . . . that Doc had recovered. . . .'
The effort to speak her piece brought on a racking cough.
'Stuck me like a wild boar . . . then took Anna hostage. . . .
They're headed fer . . .' Ginger closed her eyes, her breath
rasping like an old steam loco. Then she made one last
despairing effort to rally herself. '. . . headed fer . . .
Pueblo Junc—'

Violent tremors seized her shattered body. The effort
had been too much. Her eyes bulged, glassing over. The
full mouth hung askew. Then, like a deflated balloon, she
expired in the saloon-keeper's arms.

For the first time since his wife had been taken by the typhoid epidemic of '69, tears coursed down Williams's grizzled visage. He laid her down on the bed and covered the blood-soaked cadaver with a quilt. Then went down to the bar. There were things that needed doing.

Doc Spengler lay on the smelly bunk. He was attempting with some difficulty to get his head round the revelation that Hyram Thorndyke was the killer he had been seeking all these years. And the father of the girl with whom he was now beginning to realize he had fallen in love. It was a mind-numbing bolt from the blue. And then to be falsely accused of his murder. Trying to make sense of it was giving him a splitting headache. He rolled over, burying his throbbing head in the smelly mattress.

Ginger had done her best to plead his case. But without success. That sheriff was one pig-headed critter, hard-nosed and stubborn as a wild bronc.

Doc had lost all track of time. The prison walls were starting to close in. He was feeling claustrophobic. Shadows drifted across the blank adobe walls with the speed of a slow tortoise. All he knew was that night had crept up on him like a suffocating wet blanket. For hours he lay there, unmoving, his mind in a chaotic muddle of unresolved questions.

One thing was certain. Somehow he had to escape. There was a lot at stake. Not least his life.

Sleep eventually blotted out the nightmarish scenario.

Sometime later he was awakened by a small pebble landing on his bunk. Another splashed into the slop-bucket in the corner. Struggling upright, Doc shook the lethargy from his clogged brain.

Then a harsh gurgle issued through the barred window. Even though the sound was muted by the thick prison walls, there was no denying its origin.

Whispering Williams.

'That you, Whispers?'

'Who else talks like this?' came back the harsh rejoinder. 'And keep yer voice down. That sheriff has ears like a prairie-dog.'

Doc felt a surge of excitement. He was not alone after all.

'I've got some'n for yer,' hissed Williams. 'Then it's up to you.' A scratching of metal against metal followed as the barman pushed a six-shooter through the bars.

'How's Ginger takin' this?' asked Doc anxiously.

An ominous silence followed.

'She's dead, son.' Williams's lacerated vocal chords creaked with distress. 'Stuck through with a stiletto by that bastard Warriner. Then he lit out taking poor Anna along as a hostage, just in case he was followed. I reported it to the sheriff. But even with all this evidence, Delmar weren't for shiftin' his mulish ass. Says he wants proof. So here I am.'

Doc was distraught. He and the singer had been through a lot together. She didn't deserve this sort of ending. He could feel his hackles rising as the blood rushed to his head. This was all Warriner's doing.

'Much obliged to you, Whispers,' murmured Doc, sticking the brand-new Peacemaker into his belt. He had always wanted one of the prized revolvers. He now had to ensure that it was put to good use.

'Another thing,' mumbled Williams. 'Afore she hit the last round-up, Ginger heard the varmint say he was headin' fer Pueblo Junction.'

Doc nodded to himself in the dark.

'There'll be a horse and saddle-pack waitin' round back of the Bullet when you're ready,' finished Williams. 'Good luck. An' good huntin'!'

Then he was gone.

His parting words drifted on the sighing wind. Good hunting! A stark and vengeful inscription seared itself on to Doc's brain. He would hunt Warriner down and kill him for the cowardly dog he was, or bring him back for Judge Bodine's blessing.

Doc could hardly contain his impatience. But he knew that careful handling of the situation was needed if he were to escape the unrelenting clutches of Sheriff Frank Delmar without any more blood being shed.

He sat down on the bunk to figure out a plan.

'You there, Sheriff?'

No answer. Again. This time louder.

'I know you're in there, Delmar. Them farts is louder than a buffalo stampede.' Doc waited, sticking the .45 behind his back.

He gave a sigh of relief as the office chair scraped back, followed by a throaty grunt of irritation. Delmar had been immersed in one of the new dime novels that were becoming popular. And with a bottle of blue label to hand, he was none too pleased at being disturbed.

The cell-block door creaked open and the sheriff's bulky frame filled the space, silhouetted against the light behind.

'What you caterwaulin' about, Spengler?' He was swaying, his grating words slurred and uneven.

'Any chance of some coffee?' asked Doc, 'And a bite to eat as well if'n you got something. Ain't eaten a thing in a coon's age.'

Delmar uttered some grumbling comment, then shrugged, backing off into the office. In a minute he returned with a steaming mug in his hand.

'Much obliged, Sheriff,' said Doc, trying to keep the edginess from his voice.

Delmar took a step forward, his arm outstretched.

Doc slowly extended his left arm at the same time poking the revolver through the thick iron bars.

'Stand back and drop that mug!' A tight-lipped rasp had replaced the unhappy whine. 'And don't think about trying any funny business. If you have me down as a killer, then you'll know I ain't got nothing to lose by plugging you as well.'

Delmar's jaw sagged. He was stunned into immobility.

'Do it,' snapped Doc, prodding the hogleg forward. Delmar's brain kicked back into action, rapidly shaking off the liquor-induced torpor. He slumped back against the wall still clutching the forgotten coffee-mug.

'Now slowly pass that bunch of keys over here,' rasped Doc.

The sheriff's eyes took on a hard gleam. Suckered by a tinhorn gambler in his own hoosegow. But not for long. He unhooked the keys from his belt, and made to pass them over. Doc's gaze shifted to the advancing means of release. Just as he was reaching out, Delmar tossed the hot liquid at his face.

Doc yelled in pain as thick brown globules spattered his exposed skin. Luckily, the bars had reduced the full force of the scalding cascade. He stepped back, hauling off a couple of warning shots, one of which smashed the mug from Delmar's hand. The other clipped the wall inches from his head. Fragments of hard clay drew blood from the lawman's cheek. Not serious, but enough to slow his gun hand. The shattering blast echoed round the thick walls. Delmar wilted, sagged back clutching his lacerated visage.

'Darned fool,' roared Doc shaking the smoking gun. 'You after gettin' yourself killed?'

The keys lay on the dirt floor. Keeping the .45 aimed at the sheriff's head, he leaned forward through the bars and scooped them up. A quick go of trial and error followed till the correct one unlocked the cell door.

'Inside!' rapped Doc. He knew that gunfire was not unusual in a frontier town like Bent's Crossing after sundown. But coming from the direction of the jailhouse, it might attract unwanted curiosity. 'And hurry it up!'

Once inside the cell Delmar was temporarily secured with his own belt and suspenders. Doc then hurried into the outer office to find a more permanent means of constraint. A coiled lasso hanging from a hook was ideal. He then roughly gagged the sheriff to stifle his threatening invective.

'I don't mean you any harm, Delmar,' he said, tethering the lawman to the bunk. 'This has been forced on me. Maybe you figure you were only doing your job by arresting me. But that ain't no consolation.' The sheriff winced as the hide rope bit into his wrists. 'Slick Warriner's the killer you should be after. And he's hightailed it for pastures new with Miss Thorndyke. You take my word, mister, he'll kill her just as easily as he did Ginger LaPlage once she becomes a burden.' Doc's outpouring was laced with biting acrimony. 'It's my sworn aim to bring her back safely and clear my name. I'll bring Warriner in too, if possible. But that ain't no priority.'

Doc's effort to convince Delmar of his honourable intentions fell on deaf ears. The sheriff's frosty look, cold and unflinching, promised dire retribution.

Dismissing the toothless threat with a shrug, Doc finished with: 'And if'n I don't return, it'll only be 'cos Warriner bested me. And seeing as I'm the only one that knows which way he's heading, it'll take the devil's help for you to follow.'

A mirthless smirk cracked the icy façade. 'Wish me luck, Sheriff.'

Then he left silently through the rear door. Flitting behind the buildings on Animas Street like a shadow, he skirted around open back lots to reached his destination. Whispering Williams had been true to his word.

A powerful chestnut stood waiting patiently behind the Silver Bullet. Two saddle-bags contained basic provisions for a week. And fastened behind the cantle was a bedroll. Most important as far as Doc was concerned was the rosewood stock of a rifle poking from its side scabbard. He lifted out the latest edition to the Winchester armoury – the legendary .44-40 lever-action repeater. In later years this celebrated rifle would become known as 'the gun that won the West'.

Suppressing the thrill of being given possession of such a superb firearm, Doc was well aware of its avowed purpose in his hands. He cocked his ears, listening for any abnormal sounds, indications that his escape had been discovered.

Nothing, apart from the customary hullabaloo of a

borderline settlement at night. Inside the Silver Bullet, the tinkling of a piano accompanied by ribald laughter was reassuring to the ear. Doc stepped up into the saddle and settled himself. It was a long time since he had ridden alone. Three months at least.

After readjusting the stirrups he pointed the cayuse towards the western horizon. The animal responded positively to his gentle prompting. An ethereal moon revealed the grim cast playing across his hard-bitten visage as the young gambler rode out of Bent's Crossing in pursuit of his destiny.

FOURTEEN

BACK FROM THE BRINK

Once the town limits had been left behind, Doc set the chestnut to a steady canter. Enough to place some distance between himself and Sheriff Frank Delmar at a pace the horse could maintain indefinitely. After an hour he slowed to a gentle trot as the ground began to rise towards the badlands of the Cucharas. Looking back over his shoulder, the twinkling lights of Bent's Crossing had dwindled to tiny pinpricks in the dark void. Then the darkness swallowed him up.

All around was silent and black, as if he was the only man on earth. Nontheless, he erred on the side of caution, not being acquainted with the country through which he was passing. Realization that he was placing himself and the horse in danger if he continued, Doc hauled rein and made camp for the rest of the night. The last thing he needed was a mount with a broken leg.

There would be no fire or hot meal tonight. He thanked the Lord that the weather was dry and calm.

A flight of twittering meadowlarks woke him as the false dawn elbowed the black shroud from the sky. Soon the western horizon was ablaze with all manner of colours. Reds and oranges were shot through with streaks of purple as the day strengthened its hold. Even the mountain sheep stood still, mesmerized by the hand of a cosmic artist at work, their long curved horns etched black against the fiery backdrop.

Doc rubbed the grittiness of sleep from his eyes as he set about preparing a meal that would serve him for the rest of the day. Once on the trail, he intended stopping only to answer the call of nature.

Soon the bacon was sizzling in the pan, the pinto beans a-bubbling. Washed down by a potful of strong black Java heavy on the sugar, Doc finished off with a roll-up. The golden orb had just crested the ridge to the east when he broke camp.

As an afterthought, Whispers had packed a telescope. Doc carefully scanned the terrain in all directions. Dense stands of pine broke away to the south, stretching down towards the New Mexico border. Due west, sawtooth peaks of the Cucharas burst from the high plains informing the unwary traveller that he was approaching the mighty barrier of the Rocky Mountains.

Doc was particularly interested in the north-western prospect. That was the direction in which his quarry was headed. As far as the distant horizon there was no break in the dull ochre landscape of sandstone bluffs and craggy buttes. Nor any movement of a human variety. He hadn't expected any. Not this soon.

Taking a squint back east, the way he had come, Doc was relieved to observe there was no sign of pursuit. A loose smile softened the stiff contours of his stubbly face. Delmar was probably trying desperately to explain how he came to be hogtied in his own jailhouse. And at a loss as to which trail to follow.

Doc jigged his mount along an arroyo heading in the right general direction. Occasional clumps of stunted juniper mingled with the prickly-pear forming welcome breaks in the endless sea of semi-desert scrubland. Water was in short supply and Doc was forced to drink sparingly.

By mid-morning the heat was beating down from an endless sheet of deepest blue. The chestnut had slowed to a steady plod. There was no way he could make faster time without exhausting this fine piece of horseflesh. Sweat dribbled into Doc's red-rimmed eyes, making them sore and blurry when rubbed. His shirt was wet, stuck to his back like fly-paper.

He voiced his opinion of the landscape to the chestnut. 'When this caper's over, I'm gonna stick to using the Overland stage.'

Until then he had to press onward as fast as possible if he was going to catch up with that slippery sidewinder. Doc was certain that Warriner would catch the northbound from Pueblo Junction alone. The girl would be too much of a liability. And by that time she would have served her purpose.

Considering this notion propelled an icy shiver down Doc's spine that even the intense Colorado heat was unable to neutralize. He dug his boot-heels into the chestnut's flank.

'We've got important business ahead of us, old gal. And

146

I need your help,' whispered Doc into the mount's twitching ear. A tight snort of protest issued from the flared nostrils, but the mare appeared to sense her new master's unease. Thereafter, the pace quickened perceptibly.

In the late afternoon of the third day the weather finally broke. Ominous banks of dark cloud had been building up all morning from the west. And they were heading Doc's way. Silver streaks of forked lightning flashing across the lowering sky were soon followed by the deeper rumble of thunder. It sounded like an orchestra of giants drumming on a tin roof.

It was nightfall before the rain reached Otero County. Single heavy droplets at first that bounced high off the hard-packed sandy wilderness. Slowly gathering momentum, the heavens eventually opened in a mammoth deluge. Doc had heard about these flash-storms while touring with the medicine show. Although he'd never experienced one.

That was about to change.

He had been told that dried-up river beds frequently became inundated as the storm run-off from the uplands gathered pace. Too late he recalled the sound advice proffered by old-timers – never make camp in an arroyo. And now here he was, laid out on his bedroll smoking a stogie beneath a tarp.

When he first decided to make camp in the dried-up bed of the arroyo, the wind had died to a low murmur. A momentary lull – the calm before the storm. Like many similar onsets of bad weather, the coming tempest had its origins far to the west amidst the soaring uplift of the Rockies. Spreading eastward on to the high plains, the lashing rain came as a total surprise to the unsuspecting hunter.

In the time it takes to smoke a thin quirly the rain had strengthened into a rhythmic hammering on the water-proof tarp. Gradually a dull rumble merged with the incessant pounding to produce a grumbling roar that was rapidly gaining momentum.

Doc pricked up his ears, muscles tense and alert. He stubbed out the smoke. The noise accelerated into a pounding rush that sounded like a waterfall. That was it.

A flash-flood!

Instantly Doc knew that his life was in mortal danger. As he jumped to his feet the first wave almost knocked him flat. In a desperate panic he fought against the powerful surge to reach the near bank of the arroyo. His mount had got there first. Like all animals, it had sensed the imminent arrival of danger and sought the safety of higher ground.

Doc reached the crumbling edge as the full head of water struck his camp. The flood water must have been four feet high and rising. Grabbing hold of a juniper-branch, he hung on for dear life as the swirling currents attempted to wrench him free.

The pulsating wall of water was now chest-high, its power increasing as Doc's strength was ebbing. He knew that he couldn't hold on much longer. Tired and aching fingers, numbed by the cold water, were losing their grip. Foaming crests smashed into his face, filling his mouth. He gagged, unable to prevent the inevitable. So this was how it was going to end. Death by drowning, his body carried downstream, smashed to pieces by this deadly pile-driver.

That was when the miracle happened.

The chestnut came to the edge of the arroyo. Still wearing her bridle and harness, she rattled the brass and leather tack. Doc reached out a hand. He was just able to take a firm grip on the trailing tie-rein.

'Heave away, gal,' he yelled, 'Take the strain.'

The screech was torn from his lips by the howling storm. Slowly, the horse drew back, dragging her master over the rim and on to solid, if saturated ground.

Doc lay there, chest heaving as he dragged air into his tortured lungs, barely conscious. There he would have stayed, and most probably cashed in his chips for the last time. It was the horse that nudged life back into his bruised and battered frame. Only by continuously jabbing him in the back with her nose was the grim reaper denied a new recruit for his termination squad.

Somehow, the comatose young man managed to scramble up into the saddle. He lay across the horse's neck.

'You sure is one helluva cayuse,' he gasped out, jiggling the horse's ears. 'Pulling me outa that fix. Guess I'll have to call you Storm now.'

The horse snickered in agreement. A thoroughly appropriate moniker. So it was that Storm took control, heading off away from the lethal embrace of the arroyo at a steady walk.

If it hadn't been high summer Doc would have frozen to death in minutes. As it was his teeth were chattering like a pack of gophers. That was what brought him to his senses. He had never felt so cold. The clothes on his back were saturated, everything else having been washed away by the flood.

All, that was except for the Colt .45 and Winchester carbine.

Doc smiled through his chilled lips. Was this an ominous portent of things to come? The thought helped revitalize his jaded spirits. But without food and some-place to dry out, the reaper might still claim his dues.

It must have been around midnight when Storm drew to a halt beneath a rocky overhang. At least it was out of the rain and sheltered from the howling wind. And the sandy floor was level and dry. Doc slithered out of the saddle, removed the riding-tack and hunkered down with his new friend for warmth. The rest of that miserable night passed in a blur of half-submerged dreams and tangled images.

Doc was only too glad to invite the new day into his life. The storm had passed and much needed heat radiated from the rising sun. The early morning haze was soon burnt away by a new sun bursting forth over the surround-ing phalanx of hills. He shucked off his wet duds and spread them out to dry. His new camp was in a shallow depression with clumps of thornbrush intermingled with yucca and cottonwoods.

Out the corner of his eye a darting movement attracted his attention as some creature scooted across the bottom of the draw. It was a desert hare. Maybe a touch stringy, but beggars can't be choosers. He settled down with the Winchester to await his opportunity. It came twenty minutes later. The rifle barked, and Doc had his breakfast. He silently thanked Providence that his whispering bene-factor had seen fit to place the sulphur matches in a tin box.

Around noon he hit the trail, much refreshed and thankful to be alive. The thought passed through Doc's rejuvenated brain that perhaps Warriner had likewise been delayed by the previous night's storm. He could only pray and hope that he would soon catch up with the fleeing scumbag. And that he had not abandoned his hostage. The notion that Warriner might have killed Anna Thorndyke did not bear thinking on.

Warriner cursed. He had been stuck in this stinking miner's shack for the best part of a full day. All on account of that damned blasted storm. It never occurred to him that the empty cabin had probably saved his bacon. As well as the girl's. Not that he was worried about her.

He took another swig from the bottle of rotgut whiskey he had found in a cupboard. It had helped keep the cold at bay throughout the long night. Not that he had got much sleep. The howling gale had seen to that.

A movement over in the corner dragged his attention back to the present. Anna shifted in her bunk, mumbling incoherently. Warriner's beady eyes narrowed, the thin lips drew back in an ugly sneer. She had served her purpose. His right hand tightened on the butt of the old Army Colt. Maybe it was time for them to part company.

That black nag would have collapsed if'n they hadn't run across this shack. And riding double was no way to make good time. Pueblo Junction could only be another day's ride. Then he would be home and dry. A one-way ticket to Denver.

Still, the girl deserved a good meal before she went to meet her maker. And she could share it with him after she'd made it. Warriner gave a wry chortle at his wit. He flung an empty tin cup at the reposing figure in the corner.

'Wake up, gal,' he barked, rapping the whiskey-bottle

on the table. 'Time fer victuals. Them miners left the makin's of a fine breakfast.'

Anna sat up and groaned. The sudden recall of her situation was like a slap in the face. And even worse, the grim reminder that she was still a prisoner of that odious gambler. She stumbled over to a cupboard and looked in the cracked mirror. A stranger peered back. Her velvet locks were all awry, the pasty face haggard and drawn. She appeared to have aged ten years in the last few days.

'When are you going to release me?' she protested while attempting to loosen the knots from her tangled mane. 'Nobody has any idea where we are. You're safe now.'

'All in good time,' yipped Warriner lightly. 'Don't yuh like my company?'

The girl sniffed disdainfully.

Even through the alcoholic blur the gambler picked up on the obvious rebuff.

'There's food to be cooked,' he jabbed curtly. His harsh tone was becoming more slurred. 'So get to it if'n yuh don't wanna feel the back of my hand.' To assuage his resentment and save face, he snatched up the pistol and pumped a couple of rounds through the sod roof. The sound was deafening in the confined space.

Anna shrank back but still managed to contain her fear, holding Warriner's bleary gaze evenly. Nonetheless she stood up and set to work on preparing the meal, watched over by the swaying gambler.

FIFTEEN

STORMY SAVIOUR

Doc sensed that he was nearing the end of his quest. Picking up on her rider's intuition, Storm increased the pace to a steady canter. The trail soon brought them to a gap in the rugged plateau. Black Squirrel Canyon was the only way through the high barrier known as the Sangre de Cristos Plateau. Fluted blocks of orange rock soared up on either side of the mighty cleft, cracked and warped by aeons of scouring sands.

Alert to any disturbance that would indicate an alien presence, Doc gently nudged the chestnut into the dim entrance to the canyon. His searching gaze probed the hostile terrain on either side.

An ideal spot for an ambush.

When the two shots came, one quickly followed by the other, they caused the horse to jam its forelegs into the loose shale, almost tipping her rider out of the saddle. The harsh cracks had been made by a sidearm, as opposed to the throatier crump of a rifle. Doc leapt from the saddle and scuttled behind a boulder.

153

The shots appeared to have been close by but had actually originated some three miles further west. The reverberating echo had been intensified by a strong wind funnelling down the constricted neck of the canyon.

He waited ten minutes, but there were no further shots. It could be anyone up ahead – a hunter, the army, bored cowhands just passing time. A nagging itch below his right ear told him otherwise. It was a peculiarity that had served him well in the past.

Those shots were from no innocent traveller. That was Slick Warriner. So why the gunplay? The blood froze in Doc's veins, his skin tightened as nerve ends screamed. Had confidence overshadowed caution: had the skunk decided to ditch his hostage?

All of Doc's inner feelings urged him to mount up and ride like the devil, guns blazing. The itchy tic in his neck acted as a restraining influence, a palliative. If Anna was dead there was nothing he could do for her now. And charging into the lion's den would likely get him killed as well.

He mounted up and jigged the chestnut forward, the barrel of his six-shooter resting on the pommel, cocked and ready.

It was a half-hour later when the constricted canyon broadened out into a wide valley. A line of cottonwoods indicated the presence of water. Following the edge of the creek, Doc got the impression that he was drawing close to the final showdown.

Then he saw her.

She was bending down on the far side of the creek filling a coffee-pot with fresh water. His heart leapt, a dance of relief that she was still alive. He was about to call out when the counselling hand of prudence once again hauled him short. What about Warriner? Was he skulking nearby?

The gambler was getting edgy. He wanted to be hitting the trail. Alone.

Maybe he should just go out there and get it over with. The sooner he could light out for Pueblo Junction the better. Forget the notion of giving the condemned girl a final meal. A stupid idea anyway. Just haul off and . . .

So what was stopping him?

It was the shooting of a woman in cold blood. Even a low-life such as Warriner had some measure of conscience, however slight. His forehead creased in thought, struggling to come to terms with this novel emotion. He had never killed a woman before. Ginger LaPlage had been an accident. Goddamned fool had run on to his shiv.

But what other choice did he have?

The black eyes shrank into their sockets, tiny flecks of ice, brutal in their intensity. Old Nick had won again. Warriner snarled as the horned demon prodded him onward. He checked the Army Colt was fully loaded and stood up, swaying awkwardly. Then, shaking the effects of the booze from his befuddled brain, he made for the open door of the shack.

Doc's piercing gaze probed the immediate area, shading the glare of the early morning sun from his eyes. He dismounted, then tentatively led the horse along the edge of the creek, the Peacemaker gripped tightly in his hand, thumb resting lightly on the hammer. A low breeze rippled the dry leaves of the overhanging trees, muffling the sound of his approach.

The girl sensed a presence to her right. She continued

with her task, ignoring the interruption, assuming it was her captor.

'Don't look now,' hissed Doc uneasily. 'It's me, Doc Spengler.'

The girl's whole body tensed, hands shaking violently. Her smooth cheeks coloured. A tiny glint of hope had cast the dullness from her eyes. Forcing herself to stay calm, she croaked:

'Warriner's in the cabin. He's been drinking. I'd given up all hope of being rescued.' She stifled the tears that threatened to erupt.

'Has he hurt you?' A hard edge had replaced the husky nervousness.

'Not so far. Though he's made it clear I'm a burden to him.'

Doc edged closer. Letting go of the trailing rein so as to have both hands free, he stepped out from the cover of a sturdy cottonwood. The cabin was fifty yards away across an open clearing, backing on to a rocky butte. It comprised living-quarters and an adjoining lean-to stable, the whole being covered by a thick sod roof.

No sound came from inside. If he'd been at the bottle, had Warriner passed out?

It was a hope that was immediately crushed by the gambler's rasping voice coming from behind a rock.

'Now ain't that a perty sight,' chuckled Warriner from behind cover. 'Two suckers for the price of one.'

Doc swung the revolver, hunkering down all set to pump lead. But there was no target. A loud mirthless guffaw hit him in the face.

Warriner wasted no time on idle backchat. 'Drop that pistol, Spengler, else it's the girl that'll get the first bullet.'

Doc hesitated. Had he been alone, he would have taken his chances and dived for the cover of the nearest tree. But with Anna fully exposed, he could not take the risk of her being gunned down.

'Do it!' growled Warriner, emphasizing his brusque command with a warning shot that clipped a branch above Doc's head. 'I ain't foolin', if that's what you figure. There's a tin box packed full of greenbacks in the cabin and I intend havin' me a high old time in Denver. And nobody's gonna put the kibosh on that.'

Doc had no option. He dropped the pistol.

'Now kick it over here.' Once out of Doc's reach, Warriner stepped out from behind the boulder and retrieved the gleaming new pistol. Giving it an admiring glance, he stuck the older weapon in his belt.

'You'll never get away with this, Warriner,' replied Doc uncertainly. 'The sheriff ain't that stupid.' Although he had his own doubts on that score. 'There'll be a posse on my tail soon as they discover I busted out of jail.'

'Nobody knows which trail I took,' countered Warriner. 'They'll be runnin' around like headless turkeys.'

'I tracked you down, didn't I?' said Doc casually omitting to mention that he and Whispering Williams were the only ones who had that vital piece of information. That soon wiped the smirk from Warriner's oily face.

'Good point, mister.' His brow creased in thought. 'Maybe Denver ain't such a good idea after all. Heard tell Cheyenne is boomin' these days. I'll just stay on the train. Which means there's no time for idle banter.' A deadly sneer replaced the cocksure strut.

He gestured with the .45 for the two captives to precede him over to the cabin. Prince was tied to the hitch rail. He was frothing at the mouth. Hoofs stamping at the hard-packed earth, his proud head was bobbing like a cork on water. The shiny coat glistened with sweat.

'What's wrong with the nag?' snapped Warriner, keeping well back from the agitated beast.

'Must be a mite tired of waking up to your ugly mush every morning,' chipped in Doc. A sardonic grin creased his chiselled features on seeing the gambler's disquiet.

'Easy there, Prince,' calmed Anna, patting the disturbed stallion whilst whispering gently into his twitching nose. Instantly, the animal simmered down.

Satisfied that the horse posed him no threat, Warriner told Anna to fetch a couple of shovels from the lean-to. Then he ushered them over to a piece of flat ground to one side of the cabin.

'This looks an ideal spot,' he mused sitting down on an upturned stump.

'What we digging for then?' enquired Doc, although he had a strong suspicion. And there was nothing he could do to prevent it.

'Your graves, of course, what else?' scoffed Warriner. He lit up a cigar, adding: 'But I'm afraid there won't be no epitaph. Can't leave any evidence lyin' around now, can I?'

Then with a brittle thrust: 'Now get to diggin', else I'll drill yuh both here an' now.'

It was a half-hour later when he stubbed out the cigar and stood up.

'That'll be deep enough, folks.'

Doc placed his arm around the trembling shoulders of Anna Thorndyke, The cold hand of impending doom twisted his innards. They peered deep into each other's eyes. Then he kissed her, the warm lips avidly responding.

'Maybe in the next life we'll have better luck,' he sighed. She clutched him tightly, limpid pools filling up as the dam threatened to overflow.

A raucous laugh cut through the briefly tender moment.

'How very touching,' sneered Warriner, aiming the deadly pistol.

Doc closed his eyes shielding Anna in a futile gesture of protection.

That was when Providence again came to their rescue.

Bursting through the enclosing screen of trees, Storm charged across the open tract, golden mane flying in the breeze like a bush fire. Her bowed head slammed into the back of the gunman just as he pulled the trigger. Doc winced as hot lead singed his ear burying itself in the side of the newly dug grave.

Recovering instantly, he vaulted out of the hole just as the chestnut reared up on hind legs ready to stamp her forelegs down on the cringing gambler. Warriner was splayed out on his back, supine. Although winded by the head-butting, he still had the wherewithal to incapacitate the raging cayuse. The .45 rose, the gambler's finger tightening on the trigger.

Doc uttered a throaty banshee howl and lunged at the odious figure, kicking out with his boot. The gun roared but the lethal slug smashed harmlessly into the rock wall behind. An iron-shod hoof connected with Warriner's skull, laying him out cold.

But Storm was not to be denied her thunder. Snorting wildly, she was all for mashing the helpless victim to a pulp. Only the firmly decisive command from her master stayed the fatal assault. It took a further five minutes to pacify the sweating mount.

Then Doc helped Anna out of the gruesome hole that

minutes previously was to have been their grave. Eyeing the grim scene, she shivered involuntarily, then burst into tears. All the tensions of recent days flooded out. Doc held here close, gently soothing the slender frame until the racking shudders had subsided.

A muted groan from Slick Warriner reminded him that the slippery toad was still with them. Extracting himself from Anna's petrified embrace, he unhooked the coiled lariat from Storm's saddle and proceeded to secure their prisoner.

'Do you think we will ever recover from this?' Anna asked her knight in shining armour.

Doc smiled, his whole face alight with a newly discovered meaning to life.

'From here on, Miss Thorndyke,' he breezed, 'I'll make it my business to see that your every wish is my command. That is if Sheriff Delmar will forgive me for locking him up in his own jailhouse.'

'Don't worry about Frank,' Anna reassured him, linking arms. 'I can twist him and Judge Bodine round my little finger.'

A muffled snickering made them look up.

'Seems like we aren't the only ones looking to the future,' observed Doc with a languid smile.

'I wondered why Prince was so all het up,' agreed Anna, laughing.

'Do you think we might hear the patter of tiny hoofs in the not too distant future?' enquired Doc quizzically.

'Could be, Mr Spengler,' replied Anna with a mischievous smirk on her face while gazing into Doc's dark eyes. 'Among other things.'